D1157634

Rock Island Lines

Dean Klinkenberg

While the description of John Looney and the events of his life are based on documented historical accounts, everything else in this book is a work of fiction. Names, characters, places, and incidents either are products of the author's imagination or are used fictitiously. Any resemblance to actual events or locales or persons, living or dead, is entirely coincidental.

Rock Island Lines
By Dean Klinkenberg
Published by Travel Passages
Copyright 2014 Dean Klinkenberg

ISBN 978-0-9908518-0-6
ISBN 978-0-9908518-1-3 (ebook)

For John.

Acknowledgments

On my first visit to the Quad Cities, I walked from my downtown hotel to a local brewpub. I had a nice chat with the bartender, Leif, who I'm still in touch with seven years later. That evening is typical of my experiences in the Quad Cities. Most places I've visited I've found friendly, outgoing people who were eager to chat and help, people like Piper and Alex. When you can visit a place just a few times a year and have people greet you by your first name when you walk in the door, you know you should probably be visiting more often. I have, and I will. You should, too.

I'm indebted to Richard Hamer and Roger Ruthhart, for the thorough research that resulted in their book, *The Citadel of Sin*, the definitive account of John Looney's life. Their book was an invaluable aid as I pieced together the Looney story for this book.

Thanks to Alex Corbett for quick and expert copyediting, to Adam Ross for inspired cover art, and to the good folks at Riverwise Press for turning a Word document into a book. And I can't say "thank you" enough to the patient friends and family who read earlier versions of this novel and offered critiques that were both direct and loving and absolutely essential.

Dean Klinkenberg
St. Louis

4

Prologue

I read a story the other day about a man down south who caught an 8 ½ foot alligator gar in the Mississippi River. Biggest ever caught, apparently. The alligator gar is one scary-looking fish, with thick scales along its body and a long narrow snout lined with rows of short, sharp teeth. That snout is about the only thing it has in common with an actual alligator. I imagine if you saw a three-hundred-pounder swimming at you, you'd probably freak out and assume you were about to die in the belly of that prehistoric monster. You'd be wrong, though. Unless you decide to eat its eggs—they're poisonous—that big ugly fish won't do you any harm. The fact that it poses no danger to humans hasn't stopped us, though, from trying to slaughter the species into extinction. We just can't get past the idea that it *looks* dangerous. And that it's ugly.

We see rivers like we see that alligator gar, I suppose, except for the ugly part. Some folks, when they look at a river, they see opportunity just down the way; while for others, that same river just reminds them of what they left behind. Staring at a river can be calming, if we let ourselves be soothed by the pleasing ripples we hear and see. With all rivers, though, no matter how scenic or calming to stare at, there's always an undercurrent of danger lurking just below the surface. Some people see nothing but that danger. A river might offer a new path

5

to explore, but that same river will inspire terror when it's raging beyond its banks or its currents drag you to the bottom.

All we see in rivers generally, all that symbolism, is magnified ten times over for the Mississippi River. T.S. Eliot called it a "strong brown god", a force that moves within us, impossible to ignore no matter how hard we try. English Captain Frederick Marryat hated the Mississippi River, especially the lower reaches. In 1839 he wrote: "I cannot help feeling a disgust at the idea of perishing in such a vile sewer." We couldn't even restrain ourselves when we translated the name. Early Europeans mistranslated the Ojibwe words mitzi-sipi (elongated river) as "Father of Waters", and that title stuck. At least that's better than Vile Sewer.

Early settlers looked at the Mississippi River and saw fresh water to drink, a source of power for industries, and routes to connect their outposts. River towns roared to life with great expectations, building impressive stone and brick structures that showed off the latest architectural trends from the East Coast (and the city's new wealth), then slowly, painfully slowly, those grand structures and the town's fortunes crumbled. One generation sighed as the railroads replaced the steamboats; the next generation was nearly washed away when levees were breached; another generation packed up and moved when the bigger city downriver got the John Deere plant. These old river towns have good bones but not much muscle anymore.

The early settlers respected the Mississippi, feared its power and relished telling tall tales about it, but they loved the Mississippi conditionally. The river blocked their progress, so they built bridges; it flooded and destroyed their homes, so they erected levees; they dumped all their waste in the river and it fed it back to them, so they moved away.

Those who see the Mississippi River as just another natural resource to exploit are continually making it over, trying to improve on what nature created to suit our economic needs of the moment. We've spent enormous amounts of money trying to bend it to our will, putting it in straitjackets of levees, wing dams, and riprap-reinforced banks—illusions of power and control. Yet we react with shock and helplessness when the Mississippi does what it has always done and will always do—run low or run wild.

Instead of figuring out ways to live with the river's rhythms, we ramp up our engineering efforts, spend even more money to build our levees a few feet higher, and build more houses and strip malls behind those embankments. Then we pat ourselves on the back, convinced that we are now immune to the next round of high water, which, when it hits us, will cause shock and helplessness again and fill the 24-hour news channels with scenes of tragedy and devastation. Unlike the river, we seem incapable of changing course.

I grew up with the Mississippi River as my backyard. For the first twelve years of my life, I spent every day on the river. We lived in Brice Prairie, Wisconsin, near the maze-like backwaters and among the spirits of the Ho Chunk and Oneota who once lived there. Mom taught English at the Holmen grade school, while Dad ran a bait shop, a business more suitable for a single man than one with a family of five to support.

Our old farmhouse was surrounded by corn, but, in five minutes, I could walk to a boat ramp where my friends and I would put in a canoe and challenge the river to teach us something new. Over time I learned to read the river's expressions, how to spot the subtle patterns that told me to steer toward safety or away from danger. I taught myself how to paddle against the current, with long, deep strokes and patience. I figured out how to dig myself out of mud that refused to let me go. After falling into chest-deep water on a December day, I became an expert on how to judge the thickness of ice. Days on the river were never long enough.

Dad got a job at a steel plant after I finished 6th grade, after my sister drowned, so we moved to the city, to St. Louis. I rode my bike to the Mississippi whenever I could get away—20 minutes instead of 5—but my parents wouldn't let me put a canoe on the bigger river.

I got away from the river as an adult as I began my career in the city, but the river never left me. I worked in a modern office building on a tidy corporate campus with an artificial landscape. Every time I was stuck sitting in a hard chair in a climate-controlled room, I dreamt I was floating in a canoe on the river, the hot sun browning my skin. Every time I got stuck in a traffic jam, I felt nostalgic for afternoon hikes where my hands moved faster than my feet, slapping in vain to keep the mosquitoes from feeding on me. Eventually, I tired of life in the mainstream and started on a meandering path that would take me back to where I belonged.

For the past few years, I've been exploring the Mississippi River again. I can't wait to get to the next town, the next bluff, the next sandbar to find out what's there, even if it's another set of empty storefronts, a rhumba of rattlesnakes, or another patch of poison ivy. I love it all. And what do I see in that river? I see a stillness on the surface that hides a complex world of whirling, unpredictable currents, where murky water stumbles and tumbles over itself, relentlessly moving forward. In that river, I see me.

1

I was trying to listen to the detective's questions, but I couldn't stay focused, distracted by the bright lights of the interrogation room and the pain in my head. I needed rest. I needed sunglasses. My boots were caked with mud. Rigor mortis was taking over my clothes, which reeked of downward mobility: a cream-colored button-down from Eddie Bauer, fraying at the collar and sleeves, wrinkled from sleeping in it last night, matched with a pair of fading Levi 501s, my collective odors trying gamely to overtake the smell of the detective's cheap cologne. Probably Drakkar Noir.

The detective showed up at my motel room around noon and wanted to ask me a few questions. "Do you know why I'm here?" he asked. Yeah, I had a pretty good idea, but I wasn't about to tell him that. "Unless it's illegal to stay in a shitty motel in Iowa, no, I don't know why you're here," I told him.

He took me to the station and sat me in a small room where I was supposed to tell him about the night before, how I met Miguel Ramirez, where we went, why someone wanted to kill him. How should I know? I just met Miguel last night, spent a few hours and a few drinks getting to know him, as a story I wanted to pursue. I didn't really know him at all, much less who would want him dead.

I came to the Quad Cities for a story, Miguel's story. I'm always looking for something to write about, especially now. I live cheaply, but my reserves sometimes get low, like now. Another month like the last one, and I won't even be able to pay the rent in that derelict apartment in St. Louis that I call home.

When I learned that a descendant of a famous gangster—John Looney—was living in Davenport, I got excited. Looney had died a quiet death—unlike the noisy life he had lived in Rock Island—and his descendants have never been heard from. I had a tip about a living relative of the mobster, the first to surface in decades. That sounded like a good story: resurrecting the Looney life through a person who shared his blood. I could be the first person to find out what happened to his family after they fled the area. I might even get a book out of that.

I know a good story when I hear one, but I wasn't trained to be a writer. I don't have a degree in journalism and wasn't an English major in college. The only writing I ever did was scribbling notes about the eccentricities and bad habits of lonely middle-class neurotics, women mostly, who patronized my suburban therapy practice in search of answers or companionship.

I was a good therapist, or maybe I was just a good listener, which is all most people really need. For my clients, paying $75 an hour to be heard was a bargain. I eventually tired of it, though. The struggles all started to sound the same. I got worn down by listening to the woes of privileged people who couldn't see how lucky they were. I had a harder and harder time listening with genuineness and empathy, two characteristics that absolutely every successful therapist possessed, or so I was taught.

I also tired of answering to smug, double-talking bosses. I worked for a group practice as an associate therapist and would never be more than a billable hour to them. I ended my education with a Master's degree, so the partners—all doctorate-level professionals—would never accept me as one of their own. They valued my work in the same way they appreciated the contributions of the night janitor who emptied the trash cans and vacuumed the floor, and they weren't shy about telling me so. When I started showing up at the office just minutes before my first appointment and skipping staff meetings, I got a few nasty comments about my work ethic, so I started slipping out right after my last client, too.

Honestly, though, I might have hung in there a while longer, tolerated the bullshit from on high and the burnout in my gut, if not for one client—Joe Malone. By the time Joe got to me, he'd already had a hard life; he was just 15 and was living in a foster home, his third. Abandoned by his father at birth, he went into foster care after his mother was arrested for selling pot. She hid her stash under Joe's mattress, an act that the state interpreted as a sign of bad parenting. It's hard to argue with that. Joe was only three years old when his mother was taken from him and sent to prison. He never saw her again.

Joe spent his young life being shuffled between group homes and foster care. At our first appointment, he was quieter than a preacher who'd just been busted with a hooker. He didn't want to talk to me and wanted to make sure that I understood that. He'd sit in the chair with his arms folded and his right foot rapping on the floor, refusing to look directly at me. Our weekly meetings for the next few months were a series of 60-minute skirmishes of wills to see who could tolerate silence longer. I won. Each week he'd give in a little earlier and start talking, usually about something safe like how much he hated lunch that day or how ugly my sports coat was. Gradually, he began to let me in a little more, telling me about his insecurities at school and the beatings he endured from foster family number two. Each week I felt the trust between us growing, and I started to feel like I mattered again, like maybe I hadn't made the wrong decision by becoming a therapist.

Eight months into our sessions, foster parents number three got pregnant and decided they were about to have one child too many, so they too gave Joe back to the state. He went to another group home, a desolate institution that he was unlikely to leave until he turned 18.

On day two in the group home, he was cornered by a group of four older boys who wanted to make sure he knew where he stood in the pecking order. He got quieter in our sessions, even skipping a few. I got permission to meet him at the group home, and, for a couple of weeks, his mood got a little better. I thought we were making some progress, even as I began to doubt what I could really do for him anymore. I couldn't get him out of the group home. I couldn't protect him from more beatings. I couldn't promise him that the rest of his life would suck any less than the first 16 years.

He sensed my doubts, I'm sure. Our sessions became more superficial, and I could feel him pulling away from me. I assumed it was my fault, ultimately, because I wasn't a good enough therapist to reach him. Maybe if I'd stayed in school and gotten a PhD, then I would have had the skills to save Joe.

After a couple of weeks of peace at the group home, the bullies cornered Joe in a bathroom and beat him again. When the janitor found Joe about an hour later, he was shivering on the tile floor next to a small pool of blood, stinking of urine, shaking and mumbling incoherently. Joe was cleaned up and bandaged, but he was done with it all—everything. That night he looped a sheet around his neck, pushed off from a wobbly end table, and said a loud "fuck you" to his parents, to the foster care system and group homes, and to me.

I was devastated. I thought about running over to the school and taking out the bullies myself, and maybe an administrator or two as a bonus. I even went to a gun shop and carefully inspected every gun on display, trying to decide which one offered the most fire-power for the price. I raged and cried and yelled so much at one point that my neighbors thought I was being attacked and called the police.

Once the anger passed, I became a miserable wretch. I was crippled by depression, unable to get out of bed for three days; I cancelled all my appointments and turned off my cell phone. After several days of venting and moping and breaking a few pieces of furniture, I realized that I had reached the end, too, at least the end of my life as a therapist. So I quit. Just up and quit, with no notice, little forethought, and no plan. I said a big "fuck you" to my bosses, my clients, and my old life.

I packed a duffel bag and hit the road. For six months

I didn't look back. I booked marathon bus rides around Central and South America—30 hours from Arica to Santiago, 20 hours from Cartagena to Bogotá. I camped on deserted beaches. At first I sat around a lot, brooding mostly, trying to make sense of my life. Eventually I got bored with that, so I started reading stories about the experiences of other travelers. Then I tired of reading, too, so I forced myself to get off the bus and away from the beach.

I visited small colonial villages and sprawling cities. I toured Bogotá's Gold Museum and Peru's Machu Picchu. My Spanish got better, which led to longer conversations and invitations to dine (or party) at someone's home. After a while, I realized that I had been spending most of my time in San Salvador, Bogotá, and the favelas of Rio, places recovering from recent traumas where police armed with automatic weapons were conspicuously placed on every corner like flags at a Memorial Day parade, places where people felt ecstasy in one moment and heartbreak in the next.

I walked down empty residential streets where people barricaded themselves behind concrete walls topped by razor wire, rarely seeing another person on foot. I wandered into random bars and asked people to tell me their stories about the war or the earthquake or the riot. I rode buses out to the ghetto. Maybe I had my own death wish, just without the will to act on it directly, like Joe did. At least I kept moving. Eventually, I started keeping a journal about my own adventures.

I was in no hurry to quit traveling, but I knew my savings wouldn't last forever. I had to find a way to make some money, or I'd have to return home and stop moving. I looked over the journals I kept during my trips and thought I had a few good stories about my own experiences. I started to feel inspired and optimistic and alive. Five months into the trip, I wrote my first piece, a three thousand word essay about Bogotá after the fall of the drug kingpins, a story laced with juicy quotes from people I met who had been caught in the middle of the drug wars and were trying to put their lives back together.

I was inspired and wrote non-stop about my adventures. I began to feel like a writer. I sent my essays to dozens of magazines. Not one was published. I came to realize that no travel magazine wanted to publish a story about a middle-aged guy attending a Maya wedding in Guatemala or his near kidnapping by a paramilitary group in Panama's Darién Gap. The magazines wanted stories about the seven best beaches of Costa Rica, but I didn't want to tell anyone about the beaches I loved in Costa Rica.

After the rejections piled up, I went back through those travel magazines and realized I had to adapt or go home. So I wrote about the nine best Caribbean islands for honeymoons, the six secrets of the Vatican, and seven questions to ask yourself when you are thinking about buying travel insurance. But I refused to change how I traveled. While researching those Caribbean beaches, I smoked ganja with Rastafarians in Jamaica; after visiting the Vatican, I hung out in Sicily and learned Italian from three Cosa Nostra soldiers; and when I wrote about travel insurance I was driving a 1977 Land Rover through Ethiopia.

I became a travel writer. For the past four years I've made my living by visiting places that interest me; it doesn't pay much, but I'm good at keeping my expenses low. I'm drawn to the people and places that exist on the margins, far from the consciousness of most Americans and the corporate press: migrant farm workers, shanty boat dwellers, and the free spirits who choose to live from hand to mouth. I want to tell the stories about the people who lead big, tragic lives, like the wealthy speculator who lived in a mansion and died in a hovel, as well as the everyday people who toil in anonymity assembling turbines or picking tomatoes. I prefer the people with big ideas who weren't proven right until long after they died, and the musicians and artists and anyone, really, who chooses to live an unconventional life. I'm drawn to them all.

I've met a lot of people who lived on the edge and took ridiculous risks. I have taken some of the same risks. Someday I may write a book about my adventures, a memoir, I suppose, but for now I turn most of my encounters into fluff pieces for middle-class families who want to know which cafés at Epcot Center have the healthiest food and the quickest service or which Memphis dives have the most succulent ribs. Every now and then, though, I get lucky, and one of my adventure stories finds a home with a magazine. After a few tries, National Geographic Traveler finally ran my piece about trekking through the Darién Gap.

So I suppose it shouldn't be a surprise that I ended up on the wrong end of an interrogation. I take chances; I just may have taken a few too many last night. Did I really get in a bar fight? Were those German tourists real or was that just the booze? Who would want to kill Miguel, and why does this detective think I might have been involved?

A loud rap on the table jolted my attention back to the detective in front of me.

"Mr. Dodge?" Detective Martens of the Moline Police Department, was struggling to get my attention. "Hello?" he said as he snapped his fingers in front of my face.

"Yeah; sorry," I responded, slowly looking up at him.

"Welcome back. As I've been trying to explain, the body of Miguel Ramirez was found this morning, floating in the water near Suiter Park. According to his phone records, you were the last person he contacted. He sent you a text message around 5am."

I opened and closed my eyes a few times, trying to focus, trying to remember.

"How did you know Mr. Ramirez?"

I dropped my head into my hands. Shit. What the hell am I doing?

2

Detective Martens filled a Styrofoam cup with coffee and set it down in front of me. "Maybe this will help you pay attention," he said. He sat down and flipped through a short stack of papers he slid out of a thin manila folder. Martens wasn't an attractive guy. His face looked like it took on an asteroid belt and lost, the legacy of persistent adolescent acne, I suppose. The bags under his eyes sagged from the weight of too many years of interrogating fools like me. He was wearing a grey suit coat that was some three sizes too big for him, probably a last-minute purchase at Goodwill when he needed something nice to wear to a funeral. Maybe he used to be bigger.

"You look tired, Mr. Dodge," Martens said. "Must have been one hell of a night you had. Tell me about it. How did you know Ramirez?"

I took a sip of coffee. Yes. It had been one hell of a night, just another in a string of one-hell-of-a-nights. "I met Miguel at the Crooked Spine," I began, rubbing my eyes and answering without looking up. "I got in town in the afternoon and went there for happy hour. I'd heard it could be an entertaining place at that time of day." I wasn't about to tell him that I went to the Crooked Spine specifically to meet Miguel; that wouldn't look good.

"So what happened when you got there?"

"I took the only open seat at the bar and tried to talk

to the young lady sitting next to me, but she wasn't the chatting type, at least with me, more interested in her friends, I guess. Can't blame her for that. I chatted up the bartender when he wasn't too busy; Noah was his name, I think, in a band of some kind. The group next to me left when their glasses were empty, and two guys took their place. One of them was Miguel. The guy who came with him wasn't interested in much except the screen of his iPhone, so Miguel seemed glad to have someone to talk to. We found out that we liked some of the same things."

"What did you have in common? You're a lot older than him, after all." The detective looked down and picked up a pen.

"I'm not a lot older." I paused before continuing, raising my head to look at him. "Maybe you need to get out more, detective. It's possible to have conversations, even friendships, with people who aren't just like you. Miguel and I had similar tastes in music, for one thing. I had been listening to some songs from Iowa musicians lately; he knew who they were and was a fan of the same ones. He was also a student at Dickey training to be a chiropractor someday, and while I didn't get to pop any backs in my previous life as a therapist, we found a lot of common ground between the two professions."

"OK. So you had a drink and talked to him at the Crooked Spine. What happened next?"

"I was getting hungry and wanted to go to the Schnitzel Haus in Moline for dinner—I hadn't had a good bratwurst in a long time—so I invited him to come along. He did."

20

"Why would he go with you there? You had just met, right?"

"I didn't really question it. Why wouldn't he? He was hungry, too, and he was probably grateful to have an excuse to ditch the guy he came to the bar with."

"So you got to the Schnitzel Haus, and presumably you ate something. What else happened there? What did you talk about?"

"When we got to the Schnitzel Haus, two long tables were packed with people who seemed unusually happy. They were singing something in German and toasting each other on every verse. 'Prost!' they would roar, then clang glasses and finish their beer with one long gulp. We watched for a couple of minutes before we were seated for dinner, ended up at a table across the room from them."

The detective fidgeted in his chair. "That's very entertaining, Dodge. So tell me what you two talked about during dinner."

"I asked Miguel about his family, and he wanted to know about travel writing. Shit like that." The detective set the pen down and rubbed his temples.

"What did he tell you about his family?"

"He told me that he was from Texas, that his dad had been in trouble, did time in prison, apparently. He didn't get into any detail about it, though."

"So how long do you think you were there?"

"I'm not sure. Maybe two hours. We were there long enough to eat dinner, and then join that group for a toast and a song—I almost mastered it; it was called Eisgekühlter Bommerlunder. Those people, the ones singing and toasting, it turned out they were German tourists passing through the area. They wanted to see the Mississippi River while they were in the US, so this was their first stop after arriving at Chicago. One night in the Quad Cities, that's all. They walked along the river at LeClaire Park and dipped a toe in the water. That was enough for them, so they went to the Schnitzel Haus to eat and drink. I don't get it. They came all the way from Germany to see the Mississippi River and when they got there, all they did was look at it for a few minutes, then go eat food and drink beer to remind them of the country they literally just left."

That wasn't a lie. I really didn't get it. Since abandoning my therapy practice, I ached for new experiences. I had no desire to do something just because it reminded me of things I had already done or to visit places I had already been to. I didn't just crave novelty, I needed it.

Martens looked down, picked up the pen again and began tapping it on the table. "Imagine that. People doing strange things. That's a new one. So where did you go after you left the Schnitzel Haus?"

I sat back in the chair. "We walked around the corner to Rolling Rapids Brewery. They were supposed to have a musician playing—someone from Minneapolis who has a following here—so we decided to check him out. He was awful; we hated him, or I did, anyway—just another no-talent Neil Young cover-hack—so we thought we might have a better time at the Locked Down Tavern."

"So Ramirez went with you to the Locked Down, too?"

"Yeah. He was still following me around at that point."

"You sure got around last night, Dodge; you've got good stamina for a man of your age. So tell me about the Locked Down. What did you do there?"

"It was busy. Even Miguel's friend was there, the guy who couldn't get his nose out of his iPhone at the Crooked Spine earlier. Cody was his name, I think."

"Cody what?"

"No idea. I never heard his last name."

"What do you know about him?"

"That he's an asshole, but not much else."

The detective almost smiled. "What makes him an asshole?"

"He was all over Miguel, giving him a hard time for not spending the whole night with him, trying to make him feel guilty about hanging out with me, and making sure everyone in Davenport could hear him. And he was really drunk, so he kept repeating a lot of the same shit, forgetting that he'd already said it once, but managing to say it louder each time, like he'd been underwater for a while and needed to pop his ears."

"OK. So Cody's a loud, obnoxious drunk. What else did you find out about him?"

"He and Miguel go to school together, at Dickey, and I think they are—or were—roommates. Cody barely noticed that I was there, so I didn't find out much about him, even after he followed us over to the pool table."

"It's gotta be getting late by this point in the night, right?"

"Yeah. We closed the Locked Down. Cody was too drunk to make it home on his own, so Miguel helped him. I think Miguel had had enough at that point, anyway. I was still feeling good and a little lucky, so I went to the Blackhawk Casino just up the road and spent some time making donations to the City of Bettendorf and to the Las Vegas syndicate that owns the joint."

"Meaning you lost some money."

"Yeah. I lost some money." Gambling wasn't really my favorite pastime, but there wasn't much else open at 2am.

"So how long were you at the casino?" the detective asked, fiddling with his pen.

"I was there until I got a text from Miguel, so I guess that was around 5am. He was looking for a ride home and was hoping I was still awake."

Martens put his pen down and straightened up. "How do you know it was five?"

"Because you told me earlier that he sent me a text at 5am."

"Right." He leaned back, sighed, and stood up. "What did he want?"

"He asked for a ride home. He said he was at Suiter Park, at the parking lot near the bridge. That seemed like a good time to cut my losses, so I told him I'd come pick him up."

Martens walked over to a wall and picked at a fleck of loose paint. He leaned against the wall and turned back to look at me. "OK, it's early in the morning now; you've been out drinking all night, and you decide to drive from Bettendorf to Moline. Right?"

"That's what I'm saying."

"OK. So what happened when you got there?"

"Nothing. I couldn't find him. I got to the parking lot

and didn't see anyone, so I parked and walked around for a few minutes.

"I suppose that's where you picked up the mud on your boots?"

I hadn't given the detective enough credit. He was a quicker study than I thought. "Yeah. The rain last night was pretty heavy. I don't even remember noticing the mud when I was there."

"So you walked around in the mud. Go on."

"Well, I looked around but I couldn't find him anywhere. I tried calling him, but he didn't answer his phone. So I gave up and left."

"You just left?"

"What else was I going to do?" I sat back and crossed my arms. "He wasn't answering his phone, and I didn't really know much about him. We had just met, right? I figured something else came up and he got a ride from someone else, maybe that Cody guy. I didn't see any point to sticking around, especially once it started to rain."

"Where did you go after you left the park?"

"I was wet and tired by that point, so I drove back across the river to my motel."

"And that's the whole night?" he asked, glancing down at my hands. I slid my left hand over my right to hide the scrapes on my knuckles.

"Yeah. That was my night."

Martens walked back toward me, placed his hands on the table, and leaned forward. "Why do you suppose Ramirez contacted you for a ride at that hour?"

"I'm not really sure. He's not from the area, right, so he probably doesn't know many people here. Maybe he thought of me because we had just been hanging out a couple of hours earlier."

"So the last time you saw him alive was around 2am when the Locked Down closed, then you got a text from him three hours later. What do you suppose he did in those three hours?"

"I have no idea. I thought he was heading back to his apartment, with Cody. How he got from there to Suiter Park, I don't know."

"Were there any other cars in the parking lot when you got to Suiter Park?"

"No; I didn't see any."

"OK. So you don't know how he got to Suiter Park, much less why he was there so early in the morning, and, when you got there, you didn't find him anyway."

"That's a pretty good summary, yes."

"Well, you probably didn't find him because he was dead already."

I turned away from Martens and cleared my throat. I wasn't yet used to the idea that Miguel was dead. "Yeah," I finally said. "Maybe he was, dead already, like you said."

"You know, Dodge, I was beginning to think that you weren't bothered at all by this kid's death. You've been very...very...matter-of-fact about the whole thing so far, indifferent, even."

"I guess I'm just not good at expressing my feelings."

"I don't know; you seem to be doing fine right now. Anyway, that's enough for today. You should stay in the area for a while, so I hope you don't have any plans to leave town soon. I'm sure we'll want to talk to you again."

The detective didn't seem convinced that he was getting the full story from me—he had good instincts—but all he had was suspicion.

"I paid for a week up front at the motel, so you know where to find me."

Detective Martens dropped me off at the River View Motor Inn, a throwback motel that outlived most other pre-World War II mom-and-pop motels only to have to fight back the chain motels that spread like Asian carp. It was probably a nice place to stay when it opened in 1937, but today it defined budget motel. I paid $41 for a single room, the cheapest option in town that didn't require a tent and an air mattress.

I've stayed in worse places. My room, number 112, came with a number of unique amenities, like the boxy Sony television with dials and no remote, the orange countertop next to the bathroom, and the worn carpet that was a poor replica of oak flooring when it was new. At least it was clean, as long as you didn't look too close. The motel attracted a diverse clientele. My neighbors included a truck driver to my right, some backpackers in a room above me, and, seven doors down, a drug dealer who tried to sell me pot before I could lift my duffel bag out of the trunk.

I badly needed some sleep, but I had to make a quick call first.

"Brian?"

"What's up, Frank?"

"I think I'm going to need your help. I may be in a little trouble."

3

"This isn't a great time for me, Frank. What do you mean you may be in trouble?" Jefferson asked me.

Brian Jefferson had heard this from me before. We went to the same private schools in St. Louis from seventh grade through high school. When I went to Saint Louis University, Jefferson went to St. Louis Community College then to the police academy, but we still hung out almost every day.

"You remember that guy you told me about, Miguel Ramirez, the one in Davenport that might be related to John Looney?" I sat down on the bed in my motel room and kicked off my boots.

"Sure. I thought that story would be in your sweet spot."

"Yeah, so did I. Well, he's dead, died last night—murdered, it looks like—and I just spent a couple of hours chatting with a cop from Moline. The police think the last time he used his phone was to send a text message to me around five this morning, probably just before he was killed."

"Shit, Frank. What the hell are you doing? Look, I'm off the next couple of days, but things are rough here, with Michelle; I think she might want a separation. I have to talk to her tonight, see if I can change her mind. How about if I leave tomorrow morning, early?"

28

"What's up with Michelle? I didn't know you two were having trouble."

"Well neither did I. Apparently that's the problem. So give me some time tonight, OK?"

"That's fine. I don't seem to be in any immediate trouble."

"Where are you staying?"

"I'm at the River View Motor Inn in Bettendorf, Iowa, room 112."

Jefferson had heard a lot of stories from me; most just made him shake his head and tell me what a damn fool I was. Then he'd settle down and try to think of something to say that might help me in the future. Sometimes I even paid attention to his advice. When I was dropping into random bars in San Salvador, I could hear him telling me to pick a seat close to an exit. Actually, I heard him telling me I would be a fool to go in the bar, but once inside, I listened to his advice about where to sit. I hadn't needed him to actually rescue me, though, for a long time, not since we were in high school, in fact.

Jefferson works as a detective in the homicide division of the St. Louis Police Department. He worked his way up through the ranks, beginning as a bike cop in the trendy Central West End where he spent most of his time telling teenagers and anarchists to quit riding their bikes and skateboards on the sidewalk. After that he put in time as a beat cop, then got transferred to sex crimes before landing in homicide.

He has a hard time figuring me out, even after all these years. I'd like to think that he admired the way I turned my life upside down, but it also confused him and he worries about me; he worries a lot. It drives him crazy that I take so many chances. The world is a dangerous place, with a lot of crooks and cons looking to score some advantage, or worse. At least, that's how the world looks to Jefferson. Every dark corner hides danger and everyone you don't know wants something from you. You have to be vigilant all the time. Occupational hazard, I suppose.

Even though we went to the same schools, we grew up in different worlds. I came from the country. My father ran a bait shop in Brice Prairie, Wisconsin, which gave me a lot of excuses to be near the river when I was a kid, even if it didn't provide much of a living for a family of five. After I finished sixth grade, after my sister Tina drowned in the river, we moved to St. Louis. My uncle Huey, my mom's brother, helped dad get a job at Scullin Steel. Dad was a real jack-of-all-trades—you had to be when you owned a bait shop—so he was able to land a job as an electrician at the plant. When the company went under just three years later, dad had made a lot of contacts and had no trouble finding a new job, hiring on with a contractor. We lived in a three-bedroom brick house on the city's southwest side, an area of comfortable, white middle-class families with comfortable, white middle-class values where all the children attended Catholic schools. Public schools were for fools and poor people; blacks, mostly, according to my parents.

Jefferson's family, in contrast, only aspired to be middle class. His father moved to Louisiana—he was always moving somewhere—for a job on an off-shore oil rig; Jefferson never saw him again. He was on the rig for just three days when an explosion ripped it apart, killing him and three other men. Jefferson was just eight years old at the time, and his sister, Nicole, was four. Their mother worked as a clerk in the emergency room of St. Mary's Hospital, making just enough to keep them housed and fed but not enough to buy the latest gadgets or trendy clothes. He got a scholarship to Our Lady of Sorrows Catholic School where he was one of just three black kids in the whole school. Jefferson wasn't a great student. Honestly, he barely tried. He just didn't see the point. He didn't see any future in being good at school.

But he persevered through high school, graduated, then realized how much he liked solving puzzles, especially when a corpse was involved. So he went to a community college and got a degree in criminal justice, then enrolled in the police academy. It turned out to be a good fit. If you asked him if this was "his life's work" or "what he was meant to do" he would scoff and tell you to fuck off. He didn't think about his job that way. It was just a job and he knew he liked what he did, at least most days, and he knew that he was good at it.

He was also real good with his family, or so I thought. He adores his two daughters, anyway. I worried about whether Michelle would be a good match for him. He chased her for a long time before she took him seriously, but Jefferson knew—just knew—that she was The One for him. I told him that he deserved to be with someone who felt the same way about him. He was sure that, with some work, he could make her feel the same way. He obviously did something right, as she eventually married him. Staying married, though, seems to be a whole different thing.

31

With time to kill, I laid down for a nap, hoping to sleep through the despair that was settling in. Two hours later—the backpackers started partying above me or I might have slept all night—I woke up, sluggish but hungry. I needed to regroup, to figure out how to save my ass and maybe even try to salvage something I could write about from this trip. I was ready for some company, too, so I drove to the Diving Duck Brewery, a place I been a few times before, hooked by the craft beer, fresh home-style food, and chatty regulars, something missing from the Applebee's around the corner.

I grabbed a seat at the bar and before my ass hit the stool, Pops was sliding an Old Coot Coffee Stout in front of me. "How you doing tonight, Frank?" Yeah. I've been here a few times. "Been better," I told him, forcing a smile. At least I could feel the tension in my gut releasing, even if just a little.

Some people pray when they're feeling vulnerable, but I'd take a lousy bar over any church, and Pops is my high priest; he's a newcomer's welcome wagon and a regular's confessor. Pops is larger than life, not just up and down but side to side, with a beard that drops down to his chest, braided into long strands on both sides. He looks like he'd just as soon rip out your tonsils as pour you a drink, at least until he cracks a big smile and sticks his immense right hand out to say hello. He keeps the drinks coming as easily as he smiles, eyeing the semi-circular bar for empty glasses, pouncing when the last sip is consumed, but with the intuition to know when it's time to cut someone off and send her home. I've been in that position before, just one drink away from falling off the stool

32

but asking for another shot of River Bottom Rye, when Pops talked me out of it with a caring but firm "No, you don't need that, Frank."

Our conversations are always brief, interrupted by someone else's need for a lager or a shot of Jim Beam, but, when he's around, I somehow always feel like everything's gonna be OK. Like I'm blessed. Before I could elaborate on my "been better," he was off to pour a few more drinks. It didn't matter, though. Within minutes, the seats around me were filled by familiar faces.

"You're back," Marge called out at me, then walked over to sit on the empty seat next to me. "Good to see you. What are you working on this time?"

"That's a good question," I answered. "I had an idea when I got in town last night, but I'm having second thoughts about it now."

"I'm sure we can help you come up with an idea or two." I turned to look at Becca. "Maybe it's time you write about our brewpubs. We've been telling you to do that for a while." Marge and Becca were best friends, practically inseparable, and had been for a while, but they couldn't be more different. Marge was older by fifteen years, level-headed, practical, reserved and informal; she worked long hours to stay afloat, opting for jeans and sweatshirts instead of skirts and heels, comfort clothes over haute couture. Becca, the younger one, was impulsive, fun-loving, and appearance-conscious. She worked a lot, too, but had a hard time staying put at one job, unless that job involved looking as pretty as possible, a task that she devoted hours to every day.

Louise jumped in, "I like that idea," which was not a

surprise; she's the chef/owner of the Diving Duck. "I'm sure I could give you access to whatever you need, in the spirit of helping out, of course." Louise opened the Diving Duck twenty years ago with her husband, Carl, the brewmaster; he turned out to be more interested in beer than relationships, though. After a friendly divorce, they kept their respective roles in the business and the brewpub kept humming along as if nothing had changed. In fact, nothing really had.

"Thank you. I may take you up on that," I replied.

"Maybe you should write about the local arts scene," said Candy as she leaned in toward me, draped in a homemade paisley dress that billowed around her. "There's so much going on now. It's a very exciting time to be an artist here." Born Mabel Johnson, at age 18 she embraced the actress within and christened herself Candy. She talked non-stop about the arts, usually her own, which was a subgenre of green performance art. Her art was green, alright: she used found objects to recycle tired clichés. I have never actually seen one of her shows, but I don't need to; I've seen her perform at the bar many times.

"Thanks, Candy. I'll keep that in mind." She turned and floated away, off to search for a new audience.

"So what's new for you, Marge?" I asked.

"I'm thinking about looking for a new job. It's time, I guess."

"You've been at the machine shop for how long, maybe fifteen years?"

"Twenty. I almost didn't make it through that first year, and now twenty years later I'm still at it."

"So why change now?"

"I'm bored. Honestly, I've been bored for 19 years, but I like getting paid every couple of weeks. The company's not doing too good now, though. I heard rumors that the company's having a hard time paying all its bills; I don't think they'll be around in another year. I thought I'd be better off if I looked for something now when I have time to spare. Better that than waiting until I need to find a new job, right? Do you think I could get a job as a professional beer taster?"

"Let me know if you do. I'd be pretty good at that, too."

We chatted through a couple more beers about sports—the Chicago Bears, mostly—the weather, movies; nothing remarkable but just what I needed. Fatigue caught up with me again after the third stout, so I waved Pops over to pay my tab, slipping him enough cash to cover Marge's drinks, too. I went back to my room, finally ready for some real sleep.

When I woke up it was after 9am; I was out a good ten hours. I tried to shake off the memory of an especially vivid dream: I was in a park late at night, walking on a narrow dirt path looking for something, although I wasn't sure what. I felt excited and keenly aware of everything around me, not an ounce of fear to be had. I got around a corner and saw John Looney, alive again, standing in front of Miguel. Looney was saying something about legacies and letdowns; I couldn't hear it all. As I crept nearer, I saw the gangster pull out a gun and shoot Miguel over and over, hitting him in the head and splattering blood all around, just as a rhinoceros happened to be walking by. I think the rhino was a decoy.

I figured that the dream was my subconscious telling my conscious mind to get my act back together, to get focused again. I came here for a big story that could resurrect the ghost of John Looney , but instead I ended up a suspect in the murder of someone I believe to be his descendant. I had to get back on task. I had to get back to Looney.

I'm sure Looney would be gratified that we still think about him decades after he died. He once said: "They will never forget me, like me or hate me. Those who contend against me are not my enemies. They are my friends because through them my name is becoming immortalized." So I guess that makes me a friend of John Looney.

4

"John Patrick Looney was a complex man, with competing desires to help the less fortunate and to amass power using whatever methods, however ruthless, were at his disposal—a little bit of St. Francis mixed with a lot of Joseph Stalin."

I wrote that two years ago in a book I published, self-published, about the personalities and events that made up John Looney's tenure as crime boss in the Quad Cities. I called it *Too Looney for the Law*. It wasn't a bestseller. Bookstores thought it was a history of the insanity defense, which isn't a topic that is generally considered to have wide appeal. I thought it was a pretty damn good book. I wanted to give a copy to Miguel, so he would have a more complete picture of his family history, but I didn't get the chance.

I began reading through the book again, hoping I might catch an idea about a new angle for a Looney article now that Miguel was dead. In the first chapter, I described the arc of Looney's rise to power and his ultimate demise.

Born to middle class Irish immigrants, John Looney grew up in north-central Illinois, in the city of Ottawa. There was nothing in his childhood that suggested he was going to be a big-time gangster: he never swindled his classmates out of their lunches, never pulled the legs off spiders—as far as we know.

His father, Patrick O'Lowney was a native of Ireland's County Kerry; he came to the US in 1855. One of his first jobs in Ottawa was as a drayman—a wagon driver—for the Rock Island Railroad. A few years later he was elected Highway Commissioner, a post he held until he died in 1892. Young Looney learned how to handle the horses as he accompanied his father on deliveries around town. He got along better with those horses than with the boys in his neighborhood. He had trouble relating to the other kids and didn't hang out much, rarely played games with them; you don't win many friends by congratulating the victor with a punch in the face.

John was the oldest son in the family and the third of eight children. He grew up with other Looneys—uncles and aunts, cousins—but was close to few of them. At age 15, he landed a job as a telegrapher with Western Union in Ottawa, a job that was handed to him because of the influence of his powerful uncle, Maurice Moloney. After three years, Western Union put him in charge of the Rock Island telegraph station, so, at age 18, John was off to the big city. He lived a commuter lifestyle for a while, renting a sleeping room in Rock Island during the week and taking the train home to Ottawa each weekend.

It took Looney just three years in Rock Island to

lay the foundation for the rest of his career. He borrowed law books and studied at night, joined a literary club, and became active in local politics. He was chosen president of the Fifth Ward Democratic Club, a position with political influence in several Rock Island precincts, and passed the bar exam. In the midst of it all, he also managed to write, produce, and star in a play called Emmet, a story about an Irish folk hero that Looney idolized; the *Rock Island Argus* gave the show a good review.

Looney joined forces with attorney Frank Kelly and opened a law practice as a defense attorney. Looney and Kelly bonded quickly into a formidable team (they would later build nearly identical houses facing each other on 20th Street). They might have ruled Rock Island together but for Kelly's untimely death in 1911—he tripped and was run over by a streetcar, losing both of his legs and too much blood to survive.

In 1892, John's sister Margaret married Michael Pendergast, a relative of the Pendergast crime family that ruled Kansas City. The September 28 wedding had a surprise twist: after Margaret and Michael exchanged their vows, groomsman John Looney and bridesmaid Nora O'Connor stepped in and Father Dean Thomas Keating went through the vows anew—two weddings for the price of one.

The newlyweds bought a house in Ottawa but had a long-distance relationship: Looney returning to stay in Rock Island and attend to his law practice, while Nora lived in Ottawa where she ran a millinery shop. Looney's law practice wasn't a big financial success. He had a soft spot for immigrants, especially from Ireland, and other little guys; he took on a lot of their cases, even if they couldn't afford to pay him. While he didn't get rich as a lawyer, it served him well in the long run, introducing him to many of the city's crime figures. It also gave him a chance to learn the legal system very well, to figure out ways to manipulate every loophole to get his way.

If there was one person who was most responsible for lifting Looney out of anonymity it was the German-born Matthias Schnell, who built a construction empire in Rock Island and was one of the city's best connected and most admired citizens. Schnell met Looney through the literary club and the two began working together a short time later. The relationship unraveled in 1897 when Looney and Kelly were accused of fraud on a sewer construction project that Schnell had championed. The charges were legitimate—Looney had swapped out the good construction materials for cheap, inferior products. Looney pocketed upwards of $50,000 at the expense of the man who mentored him. The accused were all fined and some convictions were handed down, but most were overturned on appeal. Looney moved on, mostly unscathed, but the scandal ruined Schnell's reputation and his fortunes took a precipitous drop—he lived out the last years of his life in a rented room.

Looney soon began to build a criminal empire in Rock Island and beyond. Long before men like Al Capone made gangsters fashionable, Looney created an extensive, well-coordinated network of underground and illegal activities. Looney put the "organized" in organized crime.

As his criminal empire grew, so did his family. Kathleen was born in 1894 and Ursula in 1898—both in Ottawa, followed by John Connor in 1900, born not long after the family relocated to Rock Island. They weren't exactly a happy family. Cancer took Nora's life in 1903, forcing John to raise the children by himself. He wasn't up to the task. He kept his distance from them, especially the girls, and when he was around, he used the same strong-armed techniques on his kids that he used at work.

Kathleen may have been the luckiest of the bunch. She became a nun, disappearing to a convent in St. Louis, probably with the help of Dan Drost, who was once one of Looney's most trusted aides. Ursula married Frank Hamblin and managed to get away for a while, but she ended up caring for her father in his later years. The youngest, John Connor, was by most accounts a nice kid who wasn't crazy about his father's profession. Even he, though, was eventually pulled into the family business. He would pay a big price for it.

By the time Looney was convicted of murder in 1925, his empire had already collapsed. He served time in prison, then lived out the last eight

years of his life in Texas and New Mexico. He
died in obscurity in remote south Texas in 1942
where he was buried in an unmarked grave.

I've always wondered about Looney's family and what
it does to you if you have an infamous gangster hanging
around in your family tree. If you are the descendant of
a famous mobster, do you embrace that notoriety or run
from it? Did any of Looney's less savory characteristics
get passed on down to his descendants? The children of
top athletes are often top athletes. Politics tends to be a
family business, like it has been for the Kennedys and
the Bushes. Five generations of the Busch family ran the
beer empire before an outsider was picked as CEO. The
Walton family still controls Walmart. The list goes on. So
what about Looney's kin? Did any of them go into the
family business?

For years I tried to locate information on his descendants but always reached a dead end. The Looney family
seemed to fade into the broad fabric of American culture
and melt into the warp, never to be heard from again.
Maybe they didn't want to be found.

Jefferson and I talked about this a lot. We speculated
about the family, wondering if it would ever be possible
to track them down and ask them about their lives and
their infamous progenitor. Then, a few days ago, Jefferson called me and couldn't hide his excitement. He had
a lead on a potential descendant of Looney, a young man
named Miguel Ramirez who was going to school in Davenport, Iowa. That got me excited, too. Before I could
get too much more excited, I heard a knock on my door.

"Frank? You in there?"

5

"It's about time he got here," I mumbled, recognizing Jefferson's smooth baritone voice on the other side of the door. I got up and opened the door, relieved to see him in person.

"How was the drive?"

"How the fuck do you think it was? Long. I hate road trips." To Jefferson, a four-hour drive was a road trip. I've driven four hours to eat a burger.

"I need to check in with home. Give me a minute." Jefferson walked back outside and made a call. He spoke softly, either trying to soothe the person he was talking to, or trying to make sure I couldn't hear. Or maybe both.

"How's Michelle?" I asked when he came back in my room.

"I don't want to talk about her right now. Just tell me what the hell happened up here." Jefferson wasn't one to waste any time. "You were supposed to check out this guy's background for a story, not become the story."

"Yeah. Sorry. I planned the kid's death, making sure that it happened just a few hours after I met him, so it would look as suspicious as possible."

"Geez, Frank. Haven't I been warning you all along to be more careful about where you go and who you meet? I knew you were going to end up in some shit someday. I knew it. I just didn't think it would be so damn serious.

43

What exactly did you tell the police here?"

"I lied." Jefferson's face hardened. "Mostly by omission," I added. I walked over to the mini-fridge and pulled out a bottle of River Bottom Rye Whiskey. After I poured a shot into a plastic cup, I grabbed another one and pointed it at Jefferson. The tension in his face softened, just a little, as he nodded yes.

"What happened to your hand?"

"Shut up and drink. We'll get to that later." We touched the plastic cups together, and tapped the cups on a table. I took a small sip of the whiskey; Frank finished his in one gulp.

"About Miguel, I told the cops that I wandered into a bar and met him at random and that we ended up hanging out for most of the night after that. I didn't tell them that I came to the Quad Cities specifically to find him. I only lied about the circumstances of how we met, well, and then there are a few things I didn't—and won't—mention."

Jefferson didn't look comforted. "Give me another shot and tell me exactly what the fuck happened last night. And don't leave anything out."

"Fine." I drank the rest of my whiskey then poured another round. "I'll tell you about it. But first, you never did tell me how you found about Ramirez, Brian."

Jefferson looked away from me before starting to speak. "Yeah, that should stay between us. I met this guy from the FBI at a conference who was really into organized crime, used to work in an organized crime unit. I asked him if he knew about John Looney, and he did. So I told him about all the time you and me had spent talking about Looney, the original gangster. How we'd stay up late talking about what he did and wondering if any of his family ended up in crime, too. He knew about Looney, too and said he had a good story, about a guy from southern Texas that he was surveilling who might interest me. The kicker was that he thought this guy might be related to a famous mobster. That got me damn curious." Jefferson finished the second shot of River Bottom before continuing.

"So I asked a couple of questions about where he lived, who his parents were, that kind of thing, but the agent didn't want to tell me much. He just told me that the guy was going to school in the Quad Cities and that his relationship to Looney was somehow connected to New Mexico."

I put up my hand to tell him to stop. "Wait. Are you telling me that this guy, Miguel, was being watched by the FBI?"

"Uh, yeah. Guess I didn't mention that part before." Jefferson looked down at his cup.

"So that means the FBI thinks he's a crook, guilty of something serious enough to get the FBI's attention?"

"Right, probably so," Jefferson said.

"Great," I walked away from Jefferson and sat down on the bed. "So tell me how you got from those two obscure clues to Miguel?"

"I just did some digging, a little addition, and some more digging; that's all. "

"Go on."

"I had a couple of days off, so I drove up to Moline to do my own research. You're not the only who knows how to poke around for answers, Frank. I went to the admissions offices at a few local colleges like St. Ambrose and Augustana, looking for students from south Texas. Folks up here are real cooperative when you flash police credentials; no one cared that my badge said St. Louis on it. Anyway, there aren't many students from Texas up here, not many at all; in fact, I only turned up three. So for each one—all guys—I looked up his birth record and his parent's birth records."

"I didn't realize it's so easy to get those kind of records, and so fast, too."

"Yeah, well, when you tell the director of state health services that you are a cop investigating a murder, you get all kinds of quick answers," Jefferson said, unable to stop a quick chuckle. "Once I looked over those records, I found a Miguel Ramirez born in Falfurrias, whose father was Juan Ramirez. Miguel was in his first year at the Dickey College of Chiropractic. Juan Ramirez was born in Chaves County—in Roswell—New Mexico in 1940; on his birth certificate, his mother was identified as Lupina Ramirez, but his father was listed as unknown."

"OK. That sounds promising. Looney's daughter and son-in-law owned a house in Roswell, right?"

"Right," Jefferson said, nodding slowly.

"That's intriguing but it could still be a stretch. Were you able to connect him to Looney directly?"

"I found an obituary for Lupina Ramirez. Besides saying that she was survived by her son, Juan, it mentioned that she had been the long-time housekeeper for Ursula Hamblin. You might remember her as Ursula Looney."

46

"Huh."

"Fuck, yeah, huh," Jefferson yelled. "What do you think of that?"

"Wow. It's not proof positive, but it's really damn good." I was excited by Jefferson's detective work, almost excited enough to forget that I was suspected of killing a possible Looney descendant. "OK. Let's back up, though. You got to this point because a guy from the FBI clued you in, and he was giving you hints about a guy that he or someone in the FBI was investigating. So forget for the moment the Looney angle in this. Right now, I'm a suspect in Miguel's death, so not only are some local cops very interested in me, but I'll probably hear from someone in the FBI soon, too."

"Right."

"And, besides being a suspect in his death, if this story comes out, someone's going to be a little curious about how I learned about Miguel, which could get you in some trouble, given the way you've taken a few liberties with your police credentials to get access to information that is generally thought of as private."

"Right," Jefferson agreed. He walked over the desk, pulled out what passed for a chair, looked it over from top to bottom and sat down, gently. "Well what about you? How did you know where to find Miguel?" Jefferson asked.

Ha!

"I did my own digging, but I didn't have the luxury of a police badge," I said, nudging his shoulder. "It's not that hard, really, thanks to Facebook. I searched for a Miguel Ramirez in Davenport. Facebook quickly gave a match, a Miguel Ramirez who listed his hometown as Falfurrias, Texas, was 26 years old, and a student at Dickey College of Chiropractic."

"Yeah, but you wouldn't have known to look up Miguel Ramirez without the work I did."

"Of course not; I'm not saying I did. Once I was sure I had the right person, I friended him. It happens so often on Facebook, no one bothers to think about why a stranger might want to be their Facebook friend."

"Clever."

"Not really. It's not that hard to take advantage of people who don't think about their privacy. Miguel had uploaded some pictures of his family, and a few from the Crooked Spine Bar and Grill, which turned out to be a favorite hangout for the Dickey crowd. I looked over his timeline and noticed that he liked to go to happy hour at the Crooked Spine, especially on Fridays, so that seemed like the place to start. I figured I'd have to go there a few times to get known before I started asking around about him. I sure didn't expect to get lucky on my first visit. But I did. I got into the Quad Cities around 5pm on Friday, and I was at the bar half an hour later."

6

The Crooked Spine—the name is a shameless pitch aimed at the chiropractic students down the street—is popular with college students for good reason: cheap drinks, oversized burgers, and a quirky atmosphere where anything is possible. It's a cozy place. If you're shy, you won't find any corners to hide in. A few booths line the outside walls, but the center of the action is an L-shaped battered oak bar surrounded by tall soda fountain stools. It's hard to tell what theme they're going for, with the incongruous collection of concert posters for marginally famous '80s bands (Twisted Sister, Thompson Twins), Broadway musicals (Cats), and local jazz icon Bix Beiderbecke. I guess they just like music.

I walked in and grabbed the only open barstool, sandwiched between people who were indifferent to my arrival. On my right, three guys in their sixties were talking about the good old days when they could come to the bar for a smoke and a beer. One of the guys was caressing a pack of cigarettes like it was his favorite puppy. But things are different today. Now they have to suffer the indignity of smoking outside, which probably isn't much fun in January. What really seemed to piss them off, though, was that they couldn't take a Miller Lite with them when they smoked. This isn't New Orleans; you can't step outside with an open can of beer in Daven-

49

port. To my left, three college kids, two girls and a guy, were complaining about a professor who forced them to turn off their cell phones during class. The horror.

I didn't really want to talk to either group, but I came here on a mission and keeping quiet wasn't going to get it done. I wasn't in the mood to relive the glory days when we all smoked indoors—not a favorite topic for an ex-smoker like me—so I tried the professor-trashing group. "We didn't even have cell phones when I was in college," I joked. The girl next to me turned in my direction just enough so I could see the contempt in her eyes, but the others just kept talking to each other. They were as willing to talk to me, a guy who probably reminded them of that professor, as they were to wait an hour to find out what their friends thought of the latest cat video trending on Twitter.

The bartender, a tall pear-shaped man, wearing a Chicago Cubs cap, Toby Keith t-shirt, and black jeans, was standing near me without much to do, so I gave it a shot with him.

"I thought a Friday happy hour might be a little busier."

"Not really. We're more of a late-night place," he said, turning to look in my direction. "Can I get you something to drink?"

"How about a Big Muddy Porter?"

"Good choice," he said, reaching into the cooler and pulling out a bottle for me. "Full-bodied, a bit malty, hint of chocolate. One of my favorites." He slid the bottle and a pint glass in front of me.

"What's your name?" I asked, as I poured the caramel-colored beer into the glass.

50

"Noah."

"Frank. Nice to meet you, Noah. Anything interesting going on tonight?"

"You mean in this bar or around town?"

"Either, I suppose."

He tugged on his thick beard, then told me: "It's just the usual Friday night drinking around here, but, if you like music, you should see who's playing at the Cornet Club. There's usually something good there; played that place a few times myself."

"That's cool. What do you play?"

"I pick the banjo, play the harmonica, and one or two other instruments when I feel like it. A couple of friends and me play what I guess you'd call old-timey music; we're called the Feema Trailers."

"I like it. I'm sure there's a story behind the name. You playing around town anytime soon?"

"Nah. We had a show a couple of nights ago; next one's not for two weeks. I don't remember seeing you here before, Frank. You new to town?" he asked, as he rounded up a few pint glasses to wash.

"Nah. Just visiting for a couple of days."

"What brings you here?"

"Work. I write about travel. I'm here to update a book I wrote about the Quad Cities."

"Someone wrote a book about the Quad Cities? Hardly seems worth a whole book, if you ask me. So what's in that book of yours? Like what museums to go to and what food to eat?"

"That's part of it. I write about travel along the Mississippi River, so I also include tips about things like the best places to get on the river."

"I know the river real well myself. Grew up just downriver in Niota, Illinois."

"That's across from Fort Madison, right?"

"Right," he said, setting the glasses on a rack to dry.

"If I remember right, Niota was hit hard by the 2008 flood."

"That's right. I lost my home to that damn flood. Had 20 feet of water in my house."

"I guess that's where you got the inspiration for your band's name." FEMA is the Federal Emergency Management Agency. They are famous, infamous if you're from New Orleans, for disaster relief and the flimsy trailer homes they give out for disaster victims to live in.

"You got that right. I moved up here after that. Government wouldn't let me rebuild without elevating the house and I couldn't afford to do that, so I just gave up, like they wanted me to. My family still has a cabin down near Burlington on an island. It was built high, on stilts, so the government says it's OK."

"What was Niota like before the flood?"

"It was pretty quiet, except for the titty bar by the highway, but it was a real tight community; everyone looked out for each other and didn't look too kindly on, you know, strangers," he said, looking to the right.

I hadn't noticed that the three college kids were gone and had been replaced by two guys. I had a hard time disguising my surprise—and delight—when I recognized the guy sitting next to me.

Miguel was more handsome in person than in any of the photos he posted on Facebook, with a strong jaw, dark brown eyes, and tawny skin, with just a hint of a beer gut beginning to show itself. Even though he was sitting down, I could tell that he was short—four inches shorter than me, as it turned out. I nodded hello.

Noah didn't seem to be in a hurry to serve Miguel and his friend. He stared down at the soapy water in the sink behind the bar, swirling it around a few times, before sidling over to Miguel and his friend and asking "What do you want?"

Miguel ordered two Rolling Rapids Pale Ales, a local beer, and I saw an opportunity.

"Nice choice. Have you tried the Big Muddy Porter?" I asked him, swirling around my glass.

"No. I'm not really into the heavier beers," he replied. "I don't get this very often, but they're just two bucks during happy hour."

Noah set two bottles in front of Miguel. "That'll be four bucks; no pesos, please."

Miguel forced a smile and handed Noah a twenty.

"Get that often?" I asked.

"It's no big deal."

I asked Miguel what he usually liked to drink, which was whatever was cheap. He was eager to chat, maybe because the friend who came with him never lifted his eyes away from his iPhone. It didn't take long to get around to the "what do you do" questions. Miguel asked first.

"I write, mostly about travel," I told him.

"A writer, huh? That sounds cool." He wanted to hear about what I did, even if his ideas about the life of a travel writer were way too idealized. "I bet you get to go to all kinds of cool places and do risky shit and be your own boss."

"Something like that," I agreed. "Last year, I got to swim with Great Whites, the sharks, you know, and wrote about what happened—spoiler alert: I didn't get bit—but to pay the bills I also had to write an article about the seven best beaches for snuggling. I'm not much of a snuggler, either. How about you? What do you do to pass the time?"

"I'm a first year student at Dickey, so I don't have time to snuggle."

"Funny. So I guess you're going be popping backs for a living."

"Yeah. I guess so," he said, looking down at his hands. "Don't ask me to do yours, though. I haven't had that class, yet." He smiled.

"You from this area?"

"Nah; I moved here from Texas. Almost as far south as you can go in Texas, too."

"How did you end up here?"

"I want to be a chiropractor, and this is the best school in the country. I graduate from here, I got a job, guaranteed."

"Why chiropracty?"

"Chiropractic is the right term, actually."

"Sorry."

"I want to do something that helps people, something in the medical profession, but I don't have the patience for med school. I'd like to make up for some bad things that my family did, but I also want to have a real job before I'm 40."

I told him a little about my past life as a therapist and we bonded over that, then we got to talking about our tastes in music.

"Maybe it's a sign of getting older," I said, something that I've been thinking about more often recently, "but I listen to a lot of singer-songwriter types these days. I used to hate country music—all of it—but I even found a few country songs that I like, just the old style of country, honky tonk like Hank Williams the Elder. I still hate the crap that passes for modern country music, like whatever the hell Hank Williams Junior does. The talent skipped a generation in that family; Hank Williams three is as good as his grandfather and, thankfully, nothing like his dad. I still see some punk bands a few times a year, but I'm not angry enough anymore to listen to it every day. That's probably more than you wanted to know."

"You're funny. I'm with you on country music, except for some norteño songs. I haven't been in Iowa very long, but I heard about a couple of singers you might like. Have you heard of Greg Brown or William Elliott Whitmore?"

"I love those guys," I said. "I've seen Whitmore play a couple of times, one of the best performers around, and Brown is a great songwriter."

"I'd love to see either one someday, but they haven't played here since I moved up."

I was getting hungry but wasn't in the mood for one of the signature sandwiches at the Crooked Spine like the Lumbar Burger (sautéed onions, pickles, and limburger cheese on rye bread). "I need to check out the Schnitzel Haus on this trip. Wanna go along? My treat.

They have great wurst and more beer."

Miguel didn't hesitate. "Sure. Sounds better than sticking around here."

As we got up, I heard someone say "Uh, dude. You got this?" The guy with the iPhone had spoken. He looked in my direction for a second or two before fixing his eyes on Miguel. I hadn't really noticed him when he came in, but now that he had his head out of his iPhone, I saw a young man with killer good looks—sandy blond hair, a perfectly trimmed five o'clock shadow, and blue eyes.

"I already did, dude," Miguel said.

"Sorry; didn't notice," the other guy said as he looked back down at his phone. "You can leave the change here," he said, pointing to a spot on the bar in front of him.

Miguel dropped the cash as instructed, then turned quickly, telling me "Let's go. Between Cody and that bartender, I can't wait to get away from this place."

When we got outside, I asked Miguel, "What was up with that bartender? He seemed fine before you showed up."

"He's not a fan of brown skin."

"Huh. Guess I missed that. Maybe he just needs to get to know you better."

"He thinks he knows me good enough already," Miguel said.

"So what happened with your family? Why do you think you have bad karma to fix?" I asked, anxious to get back to the reason I wanted to find him in the first place.

He looked at me, then turned away and looked at the ground.

56

"Not much good. I don't think my family knew right from wrong. Sometimes I'm not sure I do, either. Maybe it just runs in the family."

7

"You sure know how to pick 'em, Frank. That bar, Miguel, a racist bartender. That's a hell of a way to start a night," Jefferson said.

"Yeah," I said. "I sure can pick 'em."

Jefferson wanted to find out what was happening with the investigation, so he stepped outside to call a friend at the Moline PD to get the scoop. I swear, he has more connections than a neuron. When he came back in the room he didn't have good news.

"They think he died from a knock to the head," Jefferson said. "His body was found floating in—what's it called—a slaw?"

"I think you mean slough."

"Whatever the fuck it's called, the slough. His body had been in the water for a few hours. They're waiting on the coroner's report, but they're pretty sure that someone hit him on the side of the head before he went in, so they're aren't sure if the cause of death was the blow to the head or drowning."

"How'd they find his body?"

"Some guy was walking by, looking for a place to fish when he spotted the floater."

"So is he a suspect? " I asked, not really expecting to get that lucky.

"Not at all. He had a solid alibi. This is a tough one

to investigate, though."

"Why's that?"

"It rained hard yesterday morning. And with his body in the water for a while, too, there's not much physical evidence to work with. They're still searching the area, but they just haven't found much, except a lot of mud. They haven't found his phone, either, but they got a record of his calls from his cell provider. That's how they found out that he contacted you."

"Huh. So what do you think all this means for me?"

"It means you're stuck for now. They don't really have any suspects, except for you. And they are very interested in you, and not just because you were probably the last person to have contact with him, other than the killer, assuming you aren't the killer."

"That's a safe assumption. Guess I'm not leaving town for a while. Good thing I paid for a week up front at this fine motel."

"You should be taking this very seriously, Frank."

"Believe me, I am. I'm just confused by the whole thing and not sure what I should be doing. I don't like feeling helpless."

Something beeped in Jefferson's shirt pocket.

"Shit. Let me check that, probably a text from one of my kids." After he read the message, he tried to write a response but the words he typed didn't make sense and the autocorrect gave him words he didn't expect. "Damn, I hate this thing. Why can't Naomi just call?" He finally gave up typing and called her.

"Sorry about that. Look, Frank, you aren't helpless, but there's not a lot for you to do right now, except tell me everything you know and let me take care of the rest. You need to keep a low profile. The thing is, they're not really buying your story right now, at least not all of it. They think you're holding out on them."

"Which I am, of course."

"Right. You are."

"But that doesn't make me a killer. And what if they don't find whoever did this? They can't keep me here forever just because they think I'm holding something back or just because Miguel contacted me right before he died."

"They sure can keep you around for a while. You, sir, are a 'person of interest'."

"I prefer to think of myself as an interesting person, thank you. So I assume that the local news media will find out that a body was found in Suiter Slaw, I mean Slough. What do you think the police will release to the media?"

"Good question. I don't know, yet. I'm sure they will say where and when they found the body and probably that his death was suspicious, but I don't think they'll say any more than that right now."

Jefferson realized that there wasn't going to be a quick resolution, so he got a room in the same motel. After he left, I sat down at my laptop to work to start an article about the craft beer in the Quad Cities. When my phone rang, I answered without looking at the caller ID.

"Mr. Dodge?"

"Speaking," I answered.

"I'm Steve DeSmet from the Moline Herald. I was hoping you had a few minutes to talk to me."

I guess the cops just couldn't keep their mouths shut.

8

I wasn't eager to talk to a reporter, but I didn't want to brush him off too quickly, either. I wanted to know what he knew. I got up from the desk and paced around the room while we talked.

"What can I do for you, DeSmet. It is, DeSmet, right?" I asked.

"Yeah, Steve DeSmet. I'm a fan of your work. I just read your piece from Panama, in National Geographic Traveler. Wow; quite the adventure. I couldn't go to that place, put my life in danger like that. Weren't you afraid?"

"Sure; a few times. I had some close calls. But I loved every minute of that trek."

"You work mostly along the Mississippi River, though, right?"

"Yeah, that's right. That's where I spend most of my time. But I've been lucky enough to travel around the world, too." I wasn't sure where DeSmet was going. Was his call just a coincidence? Was he just looking to chat with another writer? Maybe he was thinking about ditching his day job for the glamorous life of a freelance travel writer.

"I know you've written quite a bit about the Quad Cities, books and articles. You must know our area pretty well."

"I've spent a lot of time here, that's true. I don't think folks here really appreciate what they have: big city amenities without all the big city problems. Maybe you see that, though."

"Not really. I've lived here all my life. I don't think we have anything all that special going on, except maybe the river."

"Of course. Everyone loves the river. You can't beat the views, the Mississippi cutting right through the middle of town, flanked by bluffs on both sides, a storied island in the middle of town, good restaurants, good architecture. You don't know how many places would love to have what you do here."

"Yeah, I suppose you're right. I don't spend much time by the river myself. I walk along it every now and then, when the weather's good, but I'm not much of an outdoorsy person. I like bars, like the Crooked Spine where you met Miguel Ramirez. I understand you didn't know him before Friday night?"

So there it was. I wasn't surprised, but the flattery and chit chat did throw me off for a while. "You're right. We just met on Friday night. I'm surprised you know about that. You must have some good contacts."

"I suppose I do. How did you meet Ramirez?"

"Like I told the police—I suppose you already heard this from them, though..."

"You know that I won't tell you who my sources are, Frank—can I call you Frank?"

"Sure."

"So tell me how you two met, Frank."

"Like I told the police, I met Miguel at the Crooked

Spine, just by chance."

"And you ended up spending a lot of time with him, from what I've heard."

"You heard right. We bummed around town together for a while. That's how I work. When I'm getting to know a place, I go to bars and diners and talk to people. Every now and then I find someone I get along with really well, and we end up hanging out for a while, but most of the time I go back to my room after an hour or two of casual conversation or sitting by myself."

"But you already know the Quad Cities well…"

"I haven't been here in a while and needed to update my guidebook. I've gotta stay on top of what's new. Some places close, you know, and there's always something new going on, too."

"I'm not sure we've had anything new open that's worth writing about, but I know we've had plenty of closings recently. I see your point, though; it's a lot of work to stay on top of things, to remain the expert on a place. I imagine you have to keep going back a lot. You must be on the road constantly."

"I am. But that's part of the job. It suits me fine."

"You probably don't get to spend much time with friends and family."

"Just the opposite. I spend a lot of time with friends. I know people everywhere I go. I have friends all along the river, from Minnesota all the way down to Louisiana. Anytime I'm near the Mississippi River I'm home."

"Must be nice to have a home that big. You must not be very shy, to make so many friends and to meet people like Miguel. What did you two talk about? I don't see what you would have in common."

"I thought you said you liked hanging out in bars, DeSmet. When you sit in a bar and talk to folks, it doesn't take long to figure out that appearances don't count for much, that it's not too hard to find common ground. It was easy with Miguel. We liked a lot of the same music, and we both liked good beer. You could build a lifelong relationship based on those two things."

"Baseball and whiskey would do it for me. So music and beer gave you an excuse to spend a lot of time hanging out with Ramirez. What did you really want from him? What were you really after?"

"I'm offended, Steve—can I call you Steve?"

"Of course."

"I'm offended that you think I was after something, Steve. I wasn't after anything from Miguel." I really was, of course; I wanted to write a story about his life, but DeSmet didn't need to know that. "Like I said, we were just hanging out. I didn't have an agenda with him. I had a few other places I wanted to visit that night, and because we got along so well, I invited him along for the ride. I'd rather have company when I go out and explore, but it's not every night I meet someone like Miguel who is fun and who knows how to carry on a conversation. You're making too much of it."

"Maybe you're right; maybe I am. It's just that the Crooked Spine has a reputation as a place for particular...amusements, where booze isn't the only thing you can get to help you feel good. My mistake. It must break you up, though, that you were the last person to see him alive."

"From what the police told me," I said, sitting down on the bed, "the last person to see him alive was the killer, not me. Look, Steve, I'd love to continue to chat with you, but I've still got work to do, more guide book writing to finish up. Gotta pay the bills, you know."

"Of course. I suppose if I have any other questions, which I will, you'll be around for a while."

"Of course. You know how to reach me."

DeSmet took it easy on me. If I'd had the same conversation with a reporter from John Looney's *Rock Island News*, the paper would have run a big headline that read something like:

Hack writer implicated in lurid student murder: Ultimate price paid for night of Bacchanalian revelry

If I was a political enemy, that headline would be printed in a large font and stretch across the front page. Then again, Looney might have tipped me off about the story and offered to kill it for an appropriate fee. At least DeSmet wasn't asking for hush money.

9

John Looney wasn't one to waste an opportunity. He excelled at inventing creative ways to make a few extra bucks from a traditional business, like his newspaper, which he made profitable by turning it into a platform to extort and bully people for cash. In *Too Looney for the Law*, I described how Looney made it work:

> John Looney learned about the power of the press firsthand. In 1900, he ran for a seat in the Illinois House of Representatives, perhaps imagining a different path to a life of crime. The *Rock Island Argus,* which had praised his play Emmet, panned his pursuit of a political role and hammered him repeatedly on the shady deals he had been part of. Looney lost the election but remembered the lesson.
>
> A few years later he started his own paper, the *Rock Island News* and used it to strong-arm and extort his way to fortune. The *News* was a family affair. Looney's brothers Will and Jerry worked as reporter and typesetter and Looney conscripted his daughter, Ursula, to write articles. Looney ran the paper from an office in downtown Rock Island, at 1817 Second Avenue, a building that was zoned for sin. The first floor served gluttony, courtesy of the Mirror Lounge, perhaps the finest

fine dining establishment in the area. The *News* ran its operations from a room behind the restaurant, from which they peddled envy. In the back of the building, a staircase led upstairs to rooms where men indulged their lust by the hour. Down the hall, Looney ran his law practice, where he specialized in greed and wrath.

Looney used his paper as a platform to attack a rival newspaper, the *Argus*, and its owners, the Potter family, which he did repeatedly and with vigor. In public statements, Looney described his mission in more noble terms:

"I took up the fight for the people, the poor, then the underdog and the taxpayer."

He ran pieces that exposed the tax-dodging antics of wealthy bank presidents and newspapermen. Of course, he wasn't paying much in taxes himself, since the majority of his income was undeclared, and his motives for publishing the paper had nothing to do with altruism but primal self-interest—it was a tool to satisfy his desire for wealth by extorting the vulnerabilities of people with money.

In 1908, Looney, strapped for cash, made a deal to sell his paper to William Wilmerton, a farmer from Preemption, Illinois who had a lot of spare cash but not much sense. Wilmerton was supposed to be a puppet for Looney, but Wilmerton apparently didn't get the memo. He and Looney had philosophical differences, so Wilmerton tried to take charge of the paper outright. It didn't go well.

Just a few hours after Wilmerton became the legal owner of the paper, a bomb exploded in the building, destroying the printing press and most of the office. Looney owned the building that housed the paper but had gotten behind in his mortgage payments. Maybe he believed that a man of his influence shouldn't have to pay, although the mortgage holder, G.A. Koester of Davenport, didn't agree. Looney resolved the dispute by discharging his mortgage with a strategically timed explosion. Undaunted, Wilmerton simply opened a new paper down the street, the *Tri-City Morning Journal*.

John Looney went a full year without control of a newspaper in the Quad Cities, a situation that he eventually found intolerable. He fixed the problem by restarting the *News* from a garage that was nicknamed *The Roost*, a dismal place—filthy and musky, lit by a single light bulb that dangled above a flimsy oak table. Looney didn't waste any time on fluff stories; he used the first issue to go after Wilmerton, firing rhetorical salvos that escalated into open warfare a couple of weeks later.

On February 22, 1909, Looney left his office for a late afternoon walk across town. He took a shortcut through an alley between Second and Third Avenues when he saw Wilmerton standing in the doorway of the *Morning Journal* office. Looney reached into his coat, pulled out a gun, and fired several times in Wilmerton's direction. Looney, though, was a lousy shot; he broke a window or two and caused panic on the street, but he missed his target entirely. Wilmerton walked down the sidewalk and returned fire, a sensible response to the provocation. For nearly three minutes the men exchanged shots back and forth across the alley, mostly out in the open but occasionally one or the other would take shelter behind a telephone pole. Folks on the street raced for cover; miraculously, no bystanders were injured or killed.

After both men had emptied their guns in the exchange, Wilmerton retreated to his office, but Looney walked down the street, reloading and preparing to fire again until a Rock Island cop interceded and stopped him. Looney was escorted to a police station, where he gave up his gun and revealed that he had been wounded in the foray; a bullet had grazed his side just above the hip. The police declined to bring charges against either man. Looney survived a couple more ambushes in the ensuing weeks, and, while Wilmerton was probably responsible, no one was ever charged with the attacks.

While Looney ran some stories in the *News* for the pure joy of soiling the reputations of his enemies, like Wilmerton, many other exposés were completely fictional, just clever ways for Looney to add to his bottom line. After an article had been written, Looney would contact the involved parties and offer to withhold publication of the story in exchange for a modest kill fee.

He ran some stories, though, simply to protect his own interests. In early fall of 1911, Looney published a piece accusing the Schrivers (Harry was mayor) and Ramsers of running a nude beach on the Rock River, just below and within sight of Looney's Bel Air mansion. Looney also singled out for abuse Dina Ramser, a vice cop in Rock Island who had been trying to persuade some of Looney's call girls to refocus their careers. Looney was just trying to pressure them to back off, but the personal tone of the articles didn't endear him to the Shrivers or the Ramsers.

On September 21, Looney and Jake Ramser went to the same barber shop at the same time for a shave—by chance apparently. Ramser demanded to know what Looney had against him; Looney responded by pulling out a .32 caliber Colt revolver and politely suggesting that Ramser leave. The barbers and patrons took the hint and got out right away but Ramser didn't; he insisted that since he had come in the back door, he was going to leave through the back door. To ease any confusion about which door he was talking about, Ramser pointed toward the exit with his right hand, momentarily distracting Looney. As Ramser grabbed Looney's gun with his left hand, Looney fired, piercing Ramser's palm with a bullet.

Ramser was undoubtedly irritated by the hole in his hand, and he was bigger and much stronger than Looney, who needed the gun to compensate for his slight build and skeletal arms. Ramser wrestled the gun away from Looney, then proceeded to smash Looney's face repeatedly with the butt of the pistol. Looney fell to the ground and Ramser sat on top of him, continuing to pound away, splattering blood all around the barber shop. Looney's cries for help were ignored by customers, barbers, and other curious folk who had gathered to watch the spectacle. The whipping didn't diminish Ramser's rage, and he was ready to end the dispute with Looney—permanently.

He pointed the gun at Looney's head, steadied his hand, and pulled the trigger. Nothing happened. Two more times he pulled the trigger but again the gun didn't fire. Looney lived another day only because Ramser wasn't familiar with that type of Colt revolver and didn't know that he needed to release the safety to shoot. Unable to finish him off, Ramser instead demanded that Looney publicly retract the accusations that were published in the *News*. Looney agreed, repeating his assent more loudly a second time so the crowd nearby could hear it, too. At that point, Ramser was satisfied, or just worn out, so he got up and off Looney, allowing the gangster to scurry out the door.

Looney wasn't to be deterred by one near-death experience, however. He would continue to run provocative stories in his paper, and some of those pieces were upsetting enough for the subjects to track Looney down and give him another good beating.

In 1912, Looney tried to smear Rock Island's mayor, Harry Schriver, who was just two years into his first term. Looney was protecting one of his trusted assistants, Anthony Billburg, who was being charged with illegal gambling. Looney had pressed Schriver to drop the charges, so when the mayor refused to cooperate, Looney retaliated by running an article headlined "Schriver's Shame" in which he accused the mayor of shocking sexual debauchery. The mayor didn't take it well. On March 22, Mayor Schriver had Looney arrested and ordered the closure of Looney's paper, the *News*.

Schriver visited Looney at the police station where he arranged to have a private room for a chat. Schriver didn't think he could make his point with words, though, so he beat Looney senseless instead. Police officers on the other side of the door could hear Schriver demand an apology from Looney, who eagerly complied, over and over. The mayor called his buddy, Jake Ramser, who he thought might also enjoy a few private moments with Looney. Ramser arrived ready to finish the job that he started a few months earlier, but a group of Rock Islanders broke into the station and interrupted the scene. The police released Looney, and he went immediately to St. Anthony Hospital for treatment.

Four days of relative calm followed Looney's release, but on March 26, a riot broke out on the streets of downtown Rock Island, no doubt with Looney pulling the strings. Hundreds of protestors gathered in Market Square, many of whom had traveled from Muscatine and other neighboring cities; the crowd had few Rock Islanders. They screamed and threw bricks, and someone fired two shots into the police station. The cops, surrounded and badly outnumbered, fired warning shots over the heads of the crowd. The mob barely noticed, and continued to storm the station. Another round was fired over their heads, again to no effect. Left with few options, the police fired directly into the crowd, wounding several people. Some of the rioters returned fire with pistols, and more bricks were thrown at the building, hitting a few cops and prompting them to fire into the mob again. The crowd didn't start breaking up until word began to circulate that some protestors had died.

In the end, two rioters were killed and nine were wounded. The police station was badly damaged, every window busted out. Sheriff O.L. Bruner called the governor for help, who immediately ordered National Guard troops into Rock Island to restore peace. The police arrested only three people on the night of the riot, but in the next couple of days, with their confidence boosted by the presence of hundreds of troops, 34 more people were thrown in jail, bars were closed, and brothels raided. Looney, meanwhile, escaped to his home in Ottawa, then fled to New Mexico, where he would purchase a 20,000-acre ranch and hide out, more or less, for the next nine years.

10

I felt unnerved by the call from the reporter. I didn't like the idea that the cops were leaking information about me to the press, hoping I might say or do something that would give away my guilt. I knew I was taking a chance by holding out on the police, but I wasn't convinced that telling them everything about Friday night would leave me any better off. I walked over to Jefferson's room and told him about my conversation with the reporter, looking for reassurance.

"Shit. I'm not surprised. They don't have any real evidence, so they're trying to use that reporter to flesh you—or the killer—out of the woodwork. Look. We've just got to wait and see what actually ends up in the paper. They might have leaked your name to the press, but we don't know what else they told this guy. And the paper should be reluctant to name you as a suspect right now. Should be."

Jefferson wasn't calming my fears. We walked across the street to Donna's Diner for coffee and a bite to eat. After we sat down, a young woman—she didn't look old enough to drive—walked by our table, slowing down just enough to ask "Can I get you some coffee, boys?"

Donna's was the perfect diner: Formica-topped tables straight from my grandmother's kitchen; chrome-rimmed chairs with cushions in bright yellows, reds, and blues, faded and ripping apart at the edges; the smell of oil from the deep fryer perfuming the air; breakfast served all day; and a perky young waitress, Ashley, who believes the diner is just a temporary stop in her career, working alongside the 60-year-old waitress, Pat, who thought the same thing forty years ago.

"What'll you have, hun?" Those words are as comforting as a jelly donut. I never return to a diner where I don't get called "hun" at least once. I was starving, so I ordered the Deckhand's Starter: two fried eggs—sunny side up—with a side of bacon, hash browns, and two buttermilk pancakes. Jefferson went right for the Edible EddyTM, a ridiculous combination of foods piled one atop the other: three waffles arranged in a triangular pattern beneath a layer of hash browns, with four slices of bacon on top of that and a hole in the middle filled by a pound of crumbled pork sausage. If you want, you can get the whole thing covered in gravy, a concoction they call the Wacky WhirlpoolTM.

"Damn this reminds me of the places we used to hang out at in high school," Jefferson said.

"You mean like Pete's?"

"Yeah. That place had the best hash browns."

"And a waitress that you couldn't stop talking about. We ate at that place every day for two weeks during our senior year. I didn't think you'd ever get up the nerve to ask her out. I didn't know you could be so shy and insecure."

Ashley freshened our coffees. "I don't know how you can drink this shit black, man," Jefferson said as he dumped two more packets of sugar into his cup. "Shyness isn't usually my thing, but that waitress at Pete's threw me off my game. I didn't think I'd ever get the nerve to talk to her. I figured if I showed up every day she worked, I'd come up with something to say, which I did after a couple of months, but it took two years of going there regularly before she agreed to go out with me. Worth the wait, though, seeing as she married me later. Or at least I thought it was."

"At least we didn't have to eat at that place every day for two years! You were so young when you got married. Don't you ever wish you fooled around more instead of getting tied down so early?"

"Not at all. Don't get me wrong. I wish things were going better for us now. Damn, I'm trying to get my head around the idea that I might be single again. I don't know what happened, where we went wrong. But I don't regret marrying the woman I loved, whatever age I was at the time, even if I'd known it wouldn't last. And, for the record, I fooled around plenty before I met her. She's the only one who turned me shy. Speaking of fooling around, when are you going to settle down again? How long you gonna keep running from your old life?"

"Nice deflection." Jefferson finally smiled. "I wondered how long it would take you to get around to that. We've talked about this before, Brian. Just because I'm always on the move doesn't mean I'm running away from something. That old life is dead and buried; period. I won't be going back to it—ever. I've been doing this for four years now; it's not just a phase I'm going through. It's not like I'm going to wake up one morning and smack the side of my head with the realization that the only true path to happiness is with a regular job and a regular home life. I've been there. It wasn't enough for me. I'm happy now, even if you don't get it."

"Sorry, man. You know I've always had a hard time understanding you. You're like a brother to me, but there are still a lot of times I don't get you."

"I don't think this is too hard to get," I said. "I had to change things up. You know that. I grew up with this river, so I'm just going back to where I'm from. It's just that now I see that the whole river is my home and not just the backwaters around Brice Prairie or the levee at St. Louis. I love what I'm doing: exploring new places, pushing myself to try things even when I feel uncomfortable, hearing the stories of folks I'd never have met if I stayed home, writing about some of those stories. Being a suspect in a murder is one experience I could have done without, but I don't have any regrets about what I'm doing now."

Before Jefferson could respond, our waitress showed up. "Who gets the Eddy?" Jefferson looked at the waitress and raised his hand. She placed a Dutch oven in front of him and watched as his eyes lit up. My food, spread across three plates, looked like the diet option in comparison.

"Maybe we should get back to business," Jefferson said. "So we left off when you and Miguel were going to the Schnitzel Haus for dinner. Continue." He grabbed a fork, looked into the pot and put the fork right back down, attacking the Eddy with a spoon instead.

"Yes, sir. So we left the Crooked Spine and Miguel's iPhone-obsessed friend and drove to the Schnitzel Haus.

The restaurant was packed, filled with a large crowd of unusually happy people singing in German and toasting each other on every verse. 'Prost!' they would bellow, then slam their glasses, splashing beer on the table and themselves. It was quite a spectacle. I couldn't stop staring, but I was also hungry, so we got a table on the other side of the dining room. Once we were seated, I didn't waste any time on small talk."

****

"So tell me more about this twisted family of yours."

"I don't know. I probably shouldn't say a lot. It's not like it's something to be proud of."

"Just making conversation." I opened the menu, which was printed on faux newspaper with the word Abendzeitung spread across the top; the menu items were overlain atop German-language news stories that faded into the background, visible though transparent enough so they didn't distract you from seeing the complete list of wursts and schnitzels.

Miguel paused to look down at his phone, taking a few seconds to thumb-type a quick text to someone, then he started: "My dad's been in and out of prison. He's out now, but I guess you'd call him a small-time crook, mostly just a con man. He was good at making up stories about grand plans or inventions but they always needed a big investment to get started. He'd pitch his ideas to anyone who would listen, but he preferred to deal with old people. They were more willing to write a check. He had a couple of schemes that actually made several thousand bucks, but eventually someone would figure out that he was just pocketing the money, and they would turn him in to the police. I can't say that I blame anyone for that, other than my dad. He was in prison about half the time when I was growing up."

"That must have been hard." We ordered dinner and continued to talk, trying not be distracted by the toasts and clanking that spilled across the room.

"It sucked. It's not like he was a young man, either. He married my mom—his second wife—when he was 50."

"So how much time did you spend with him when you were growing up?"

"Not much. Mom refused to bring me along when she visited him in prison, so I just talked with him on the phone a few times a year. When he was home, he tried to do stuff with me, but it's not exactly as if he was the playing-catch kind of father; he never even got me a baseball glove. At least he got me this necklace."

Miguel reached under his shirt and pulled out a necklace with a silver crucifix. "If you look on the back, it's got the initials JR carved into it; my dad's. His mother gave it to him when he was a kid, and he wanted me to have it, so I'd think of him when he was away. I know it sounds kinda corny, but it worked. Every time I look at it, I think about him, miss him, truthfully."

"That doesn't sound corny to me at all," I said. "It's sweet."

Miguel looked embarrassed. "Anyway, like I said, he didn't teach me much. He really just wanted me to know what he knew, which was about how to read people and spot their weaknesses. He thought that, even if I didn't choose the same career he did, that I would be better off if I could read people and understand their faults, to take advantage of them, I suppose."

"And how have you done with that?"

"I was never as good as my father at those things."

A tall young man in lederhosen brought out our food, so we changed the topic to lighter fare, like speculating on the background of the people singing and toasting loudly, and wondering exactly what they were singing. After we cleaned our plates, they caught us staring at them and waved us over. I looked at Miguel; he just shrugged his shoulders and said "Why not?" So we grabbed our beer and walked over to meet them.

They were lined up family style, twenty in a row, at a series of tables pushed one against the other. They sat next to an exposed brick wall that was lined with shelves packed with antique beer steins and underneath a mural of the Bavarian countryside that depicted maidens milking cows in front of a fairy-tale castle that looked like Neuschwanstein. We squeezed in between a couple of plus-size ladies and everyone raised their mugs and welcomed us with a loud prost and a shower of lager. They started into a song called Eisgekühlter Bommerlunder, going slow to teach us the words. The first verse wasn't too complicated:

> Eisgekühlter Bommerlunder -
> Bommerlunder eisgekühlt.
> Eisgekühlter Bommerlunder -
> Bommerlunder eisgekühlt.

There were other verses, but that's as far as we got.

Learning the lyrics in German was hard enough, but part of the shtick is to sing each verse faster and faster. I couldn't really keep up with the pace of the singing—or drinking—but I had a hell of a time trying, and I'm pretty sure Miguel did, too.

The whole group was from Bonn, taking a tour of America. This was their first stop, and they missed home already. I guess they didn't travel much. After they dipped a toe in the Mississippi River at Davenport, in LeClaire Park, they went right to the Schnitzel Haus for dinner. Very gracious people. We stuck around for another beer, to get a little more practice with the song, of course.

As we got up to leave, Miguel said to me: "I guess this is kinda what my family was like. I've heard stories from my dad about the old days. My granddad was Irish, but I never met him. I figured he must have known a lot of drinking songs, being Irish and all, and since he owned a couple of bars."

"Yeah, I bet he knew a few drinking songs. Was your granddad from Texas, too?"

"Not really. He died there, but he spent most of his life up here."

"Really? Up here, as in the Quad Cities?"

"Yeah. His bars were in Rock Island."

"That's pretty cool, that he was from here and now you've come back to the same area."

"I guess so. So where do you want to go next?"

I smiled and thought about it a minute, then suggested we go around the corner to the Rolling Rapids Brewpub. He liked the idea.

"I've done some reading about the Quad Cities.

Maybe I've heard of your granddad. What was his name?"

"Looney; John Looney."

I turned away so he couldn't see the mile-wide grin on my face.

"Have you heard of him?"

"Yeah. I've heard the name before."

11

Donna's Diner was clearing out as we finished eating. Jefferson swallowed three Tums for dessert, then we walked back to the motel. As we approached I saw a man in a black polo shirt, tan pants, and dark sunglasses walking toward my room. I figured that the FBI had finally decided to visit me. I was right.

"Wish me luck," I said before walking over to greet the man, not sure whether I should be worried or relieved.

"Mr. Dodge? I'm Agent Starck, from the FBI. I'd like to ask you a few questions."

"Sure. Why not? I've got nothing else going on. Do you want to go somewhere to talk or will this do?" I asked, pointing to my motel room. He said it would do.

Starck was trim and a little under six feet tall. I didn't see a single wrinkle on him, either in his clothes or on his face. His hair was thin and wiry, like a porcupine. I wanted to pluck out a strand and make a quill.

When we got in my room, he looked around for a place to sit. "I only have one chair. Sorry."

He walked across the room, picked up the chair and tapped it on the floor a couple of times, forcing one leg loose. "That's OK," he said. "I can stand. I hear you had a conversation with the Moline police already." He asked without looking at me; he was too busy scanning the room from top to bottom.

"Yeah," I answered. "Highlight of my week, but I'm not sure I'd call it a conversation."

"Well, now you get to talk to me, too." He turned to face me.

"Lucky me. Two highlights in one week."

"I'd like to hear more about your relationship with Mr. Ramirez."

"I wouldn't exactly say we had a relationship," I responded. "I knew him for just one night before he died."

"How exactly did you meet?" He went back to looking around the room, but more casually this time.

I let out a loud sigh. "I already told the Moline police the whole story. Do I really have to tell it again? Don't you guys talk to each other?" I really didn't want to have to go over the whole night again. It's hard to keep track of what you've said when you're trying not to say a lot.

"Yeah, I'd like you to tell me, too," Starck said.

"We met at the Crooked Spine. I went there for a beer. He sat next to me. We talked. We had a lot in common, so we hung out most of the night, ate dinner at the Schnitzel Haus and got drinks at a couple of places. He went home and I went to a casino, then he turned up dead. That's about what I know."

Starck looked back in my direction and stood silently for a moment, like he was trying to stop himself from saying something that could get in the way of a promotion down the road. "Look. I know you've been through this once already, but I need to go through it with you, too. I'm sorry about that. If you feel inconvenienced, though, imagine how much worse it is for Ramirez. If you cooperate, we'll both get on with our day a lot quicker."

84

I gave him a quick nod. "Sorry. Go on."

"When was the last time you talked to Ramirez?"

"We said good-bye sometime before 2am when we left the Locked Down Bar. He left with a guy named Cody—that was the guy with the iPhone from the Crooked Spine who I mentioned to the Moline cops—and I went to a casino. That was the last time I talked to Miguel."

"Isn't it also true that he sent you a text message a little while later?"

"The last time we talked was at the Locked Down, but yes, he sent me a text around 5am. I'm a little confused about something, Agent Starck. Why is the FBI investigating a local murder case? Isn't this a little out of your jurisdiction?"

Starck put a piece of gum in his mouth, carefully folding the wrapper and placing it back in his pocket. "We've had an interest in Mr. Ramirez for a while, so naturally we'd like to know who killed him and why. But that's not your concern. I know this must be confusing for you, and you're probably still feeling shock over Miguel's death, but it's important that you stay focused on my questions right now. I need you to tell me everything you remember about that night. We're going to sort this out, believe me, because, unlike the Moline cops, the FBI knows what it's doing."

"If you're as good as you say, then I have nothing to worry about, because I didn't kill him."

"Then you have nothing to fear, Mr. Dodge. And, for the record, I'm inclined to believe you. So are you ready to continue?"

"Sure."

"Tell me more about this friend you mentioned, the one that Miguel left with; Cody something?"

"I really don't know much about him. They were friends from school and roommates, but that's about all I know."

"How much time did you spend with Cody?"

"Not too much. He and Miguel showed up together at the Crooked Spine, and when we got to the Locked Down, Cody was there, too. "

"So what did Mr. Ramirez tell you about Cody? How did they meet? How long have they known each other?" He pulled a small notebook out of his back pocket and made a couple of notes.

"Not much, really," I hesitated before continuing, wondering how much I should speculate about their relationship. "I could sense a chill between them. Miguel didn't say anything about it, but when we left the Crooked Spine, Cody expected Miguel to pay the tab, which he already had. Cody then asked, demanded, really, that Miguel leave the change."

"Did Ramirez comply?"

"Yes, he did, but he wasn't happy about it. Is Cody a suspect?"

"I don't know, yet. I'm just trying to figure out who knew Ramirez and who might have wanted to get rid of him. So Ramirez was paying for Cody's drinks at the Crooked Spine. What about at the other bar, the Locked Up was it, was Ramirez still buying there?"

"Locked Down, actually. Like I said, things seemed cool between them, like they were barely tolerating each other. When we walked in, Miguel was annoyed to see Cody at the bar, but he went over to say hi anyway. I bought the first round for the three of us, but Miguel may have bought him a drink or two later; I wasn't really paying attention. We couldn't shake Cody after that. He even hung around us when we went in another room to play pool."

"Did Cody play, too?"

"No. He just watched. And drank. He was pretty drunk by the time the bar closed, so Miguel felt like he had to take him home. That's when we exchanged numbers. I told Miguel that I'd be around for a few days, so we made vague plans to hang out again. That's the last time I talked to him."

"So is Cody the guy you clocked?" Agent Starck asked.

I was surprised he knew about that. No one from the Moline Police Department asked me about it. "Yeah, I punched Cody. He was drunk and saying stupid things, and I was drunk and had a short fuse."

"What did he say to set you off?" he asked.

I sighed. "Look. It's gonna sound dumb now. He'd been obnoxious since we got to the Locked Down, acting like a TV talking head in search of something to rage against. He kept calling Miguel his bitch and heckled us while we were shooting pool. Just wouldn't shut up. Miguel ignored him, and I bit my tongue for as long as I could, but I was getting pissed. I figured Miguel knew best how to handle him. But then he starting ragging on the Mississippi River—he'd heard me talk about the work I do—calling it a filthy fucking sewer and calling river towns cesspools full of degenerates or something like that. I'd had enough of his incessant bullshit at that point. So I punched him."

"He harassed your friend non-stop and you didn't do anything, but when he insulted the Mississippi you leveled him?" Starck's face twitched, like he was trying hard to stop himself from smirking.

"So I'm an idiot. But I care about that river more than I care about most people, and I don't take well to people who rag on it. And, again, it's a bit of a stretch to call Miguel my friend; we'd only been hanging out for a few hours."

"So what exactly did you do, to Cody?"

"I just reacted, OK? When he said those things about the river, I just reacted. He was standing to my left, so I turned a little and threw a right hook. I hit him square on the cheek. He'd had a lot to drink, like I said, so his legs gave out quickly and he fell to the ground with a very pleasing 'thud.' I probably should have been kicked out of the bar at that point, but Cody had been so obnoxious to everyone, that folks looked the other way. Everyone but Miguel, anyway. I'm pretty sure he smiled when I hit Cody, but seeing him fall to the ground made Miguel feel even more responsible for him, so he decided he had to leave and get Cody home. Cody, as you might expect, didn't have anything else to say on the way out. When they left, I walked over to the bar to apologize, but the bartender just smiled and handed me another beer, on the house. I stuck around until they closed, maybe another half hour, then went to the casino."

"And you didn't talk to Ramirez again."

"No."

"What about that text message. What did he want?"

"A ride home. He said he was at Suiter Park and wondered if I would give him a ride home. That's all."

"Is that when you got mud on your boots?" he asked as he glanced over to the corner of my room.

Shit. I still hadn't cleaned them. "Like I told the Moline cops, I went to Suiter Park to pick up Miguel, but when I got there I didn't see anyone, so I got out and walked around, to see if I could find him. I didn't, and when I tried to call him, he didn't answer his phone, so I left."

"That's what you told the Moline police. So there was nothing else in that message from Ramirez?"

"No."

"One more thing. What was the first place you said you went to?"

"The Crooked Spine?"

"Right. The Crooked Spine. Did you talk to a bartender there, a guy named Noah Smith?"

"Sure. We chatted before Miguel got there. Why?"

"Did he say anything about Ramirez?"

"Not that I remember."

"Nothing at all?"

"All I remember is that he didn't seem to care for Miguel, for whatever reason. I noticed that he was slow to serve him when he got there." I stopped to think back through the night. "There was one other thing. When Miguel paid for the two beers, Noah made some crack about not accepting pesos, but I didn't think anything of it at the time."

"OK." Starck slipped the notebook in a back pocket. "Some of the customers said the two didn't always see eye-to-eye. That's all. Just curious if you saw anything." He glanced down at his watch. "I think that's a good start, Dodge. I don't have any other questions right now."

"Thanks for stopping by. I'm sure we'll be seeing each other again soon."

Agent Starck started toward the door, then turned back to look at me. "Yes. We will. By the way, I'd get those cleaned, if I was you," he said as he pointed toward my boots. "Mississippi mud can be a bitch to remove; I hear it can leave a nasty stain. Funny thing about Suiter Park. I didn't see any mud around the parking lot when I went there. It looked like the whole thing was gravel to me." With that, he walked out the door.

After Agent Starck left, I walked over to Jefferson's room and knocked on the door.

"I know that guy," he told me.

"Agent Starck?" I asked.

"Yeah, Agent Starck. He's the one who tipped me off about Miguel being related to Looney."

12

"Starck is the FBI agent who tipped you off? Is that a bad sign? Am I in bigger trouble than we thought?"

"Nah. If he was the agent in charge of keeping an eye on him, why wouldn't he show up when Miguel turned up dead? He wouldn't be doing his job if he didn't."

"I suppose so. Tell me again how you met him?"

"Let's go inside first." When we got in his room Jefferson handed me a beer, a Bud Light.

"That all you got?" I asked. "I hate this watery crap."

"That's all I got, yeah. Drink it and shut up."

"Fine. So tell me about Starck."

"A couple of months ago, I went to a conference in Houston, the International Society for Organized Crime Interdiction. I really wanted to go, needed a break. I'd had a couple of big cases, high profile cases, that had me working night and day, so I was spent. I couldn't convince my boss that the department should pay for it, so I went on my own dime."

"I guess St. Louis hasn't had to deal with organized crime since the Lebanese and Italian syndicates were busted."

"Not really. We got plenty of drug gangs in St. Louis, but that's a different conference. That would be work. Old-fashioned organized crime, though, that's my hobby."

"Here's to hobbies," I said, then we clinked our beer cans and tapped them on the table.

"The conference wasn't all that crowded. Organized crime isn't on the radar much these days; everyone's too busy fighting terrorists and those drug gangs. I went to a couple of real boring sessions in the morning—professors with no real experience outside of reading books—but the first afternoon session had promise: Crime Syndicates: Yesterday, Today, and Tomorrow. Everyone on the panel was a cop; Starck was one of them. His talk was mostly about the history of organized crime, how it really got started, that kind of thing. After it was over, I went up to talk to him."

****

"Excuse me, Agent Starck? Can I bug you with a couple of questions?"

"Sure. What can I do for you?"

"I'm Brian Jefferson, St. Louis PD, Homicide Division."

"St. Louis? We don't have much activity up there from what I know, other than the drug gangs."

"You're right. This is more of a personal interest. In your talk, you went into the big city gangsters, like Capone in Chicago and Lucky Luciano in New York. Are you familiar with John Looney, from Rock Island, Illinois?"

"Not many people go that far back. You know your history," Starck said.

"Thanks. So how much do you know about Looney?"

92

"I know a few things. He's more responsible for the structure of organized crime in the 20th century than anyone else. He created a network across the Midwest to move stolen cars, booze, and prostitutes, well before guys like Capone came along. He ran a tight ship, and didn't tolerate dissension. You didn't want to cross him. But he was also impulsive, didn't always plan ahead or think through the consequences of his actions. That was his undoing, in my opinion."

"That's as good a summary as I've heard. He may have been our country's first big-time gangster, but he also took a big fall."

"They all do. No one can stay on top of a criminal enterprise like that forever. Eventually they get taken down, either by an informant who turns them into the police, maybe someone they pissed off, or they get taken down from the inside, by someone with ambition or someone with a grudge. And like Looney, their own failings usually play a big part, too."

"He didn't leave much of a trail after he got out of prison. Do you know if he has any family still living?"

"I haven't really spent the time trying to find out, but I don't think so. If there are any relatives, they've stayed out of trouble, or else I'd know about it. I've worked in organized crime at the FBI for a while. I know what's going on in the whole country, and I don't remember ever hearing Looney's name mentioned."

"Huh. I guess that's a good thing."

"Is there anything else you wanted to ask?"

"One more thing. I've got this friend, a therapist, I mean a writer—he used to be a therapist. We've had a lot of late night arguments about gangsters and their families. I think most of them, the kids of gangsters, end up being crooked, but Frank, the writer, thinks most aren't, or that they don't have to be, that they can choose to stay away from that life. He was a therapist, after all. You've worked in this field for a while. What do you think?"

"You and your friend have a strange hobby. Well, I'd say that I agree more with you. If you come from a good family, like I did, you learn right from wrong and you grow up to be a responsible adult. If you come from a crooked family, though, it's in your genes and it's what you've been taught; that's two strikes against you. I don't think many people can rise above a bad family background. You are who you are."

"Thanks. Frank's always been an optimist; he'd feel differently if he saw the shit we see every day."

"That's right. I have a good example for you. Have you ever seen *The Godfather*?" Starck asked.

"Of course."

"You remember the basic story. In the first movie, the good son, Michael, goes to college. Vito Corleone is trying to shield him, give him a way out of the family business. Sonny is the one who's supposed to inherit the leadership role, and he looks like he's best suited for it, too. Ultimately, of course, Michael takes over, throws aside any pretense that he can be anything other than the gangster his father was. I know this story was fiction, but I can't tell you how many times I've seen it happen in real life. In fact, it's the good son that you really have to beware of in a family like that, he's usually the one who is smart and patient enough to be a great crook. Is there anything else you want to ask, Jefferson?"

"No. I think that's it. Thanks, Agent."

In the evening, when I was heading out for dinner, I saw Starck again, this time in the hotel lobby. What a place—fountains, Oriental rugs, antique chairs; I really felt out of place.

Starck had changed out of his suit and into jeans and a nice shirt. When he saw me, he waved me over.

"Hey, St. Louis. What's your name, again?"

"Jefferson, Brian Jefferson."

"Right. Jefferson." He looked around the lobby, then leaned in close to me. "Look, I didn't want to say anything about this when we were in the meeting room, but I know more about Looney's family than I told you before. I can't say much, because there's an on-going investigation, but we've been watching a young man from south Texas who might interest you."

"Alright. What can you tell me about him?"

"I can't say much, I shouldn't even be saying this much, but his family has roots in New Mexico; the kid's going to college now in the Quad Cities. You must know where that is if you know about Rock Island."

"Sure do."

"I wish I could tell you more, but I have a feeling you're pretty resourceful, that you can take it from here. You can tell your friend, the writer—what's his name?"

"Frank Dodge."

"Right, Frank Dodge. You can tell him what I've told you, just don't mention that you heard any of this from me. Good luck."

****

"That's how I met him, how I got the tip. Didn't see him again until just now."

"Damn. He really didn't give you a lot to go on. So what's this crap about me being an optimist? That might have been true a few years ago, but I'm not sure that I see myself that way now."

"I hear what you're saying, brother; just don't believe you. You may be wounded, but you're still an optimist, or you wouldn't be taking the chances you do. With the mess you're in, now would be a good time to find some of that patented Frank Dodge optimism, too."

13

Jefferson decided to chase down Agent Starck and a couple of leads. I sat down to write but every time I got started on a sentence, I thought of something I needed to look up, and I'd get lost searching the Internet. After an hour of staring at news sites, porn, and an empty page in Word, I realized I needed to get off my ass and do something different. I needed to get near the river. I didn't have a boat handy, so instead I changed clothes and went for a run down to Davenport, along the riverfront trail.

The Mississippi River at LeClaire, Iowa makes a sharp turn to the west and, before the US government built a dam in the 1930s, the river narrowed into 14 miles of rapids. In the early years of steamboat travel boats passing through the area had to lighten up by unloading their goods when they reached those rapids. While the cargo was transported by land to the other end of the rapids, a local pilot, a rapids pilot, guided the boat across the treacherous waters to reunite it with its cargo. This forced portage created good business opportunities at both ends of the rapids, bringing to life cities like Rock Island, Davenport, and LeClaire, even as it slowed the boats trying to pass by.

As river traffic grew and more folks moved to the Upper Mississippi, those rapids looked like a bigger and bigger obstacle. As early as 1837, a young Lieutenant,

Robert E. Lee, arrived in the area to survey the rapids and proposed a plan to blast a path through the boulders. Lee didn't get far—funding for the work was withdrawn within a year—and other ideas were proposed and abandoned until the 1930s when the US Congress authorized the Army Corps of Engineers to build a series of locks and dams from Hastings, Minnesota to St. Louis; one result of the project was that hazards like those rapids disappeared as water levels went up, ensuring a minimum nine-foot deep channel for navigation for 630 miles of the upper river. Lock and Dam #15 at Rock Island was the first one that opened. The boulders are still down there, but they'll stay buried under several feet of water as long as the dam is in place. And while the locks and dams have been a boon to commercial shipping interests (especially since the taxpayers shoulder almost all of the expenses to build and maintain the system), those dams have taken a big toll on the river's ecosystem.

The rapids may have been a bane for boats in the 19th century but companies that wanted to build factories saw the fast, shallow water as fuel for a boom. Water power helped spur the growth of factories along the banks of the river—John Deere's plow works, lumber mills, and more. Those factories needed workers, and immigrants poured into the region to answer the call: Belgians and Swedes around Moline, Germans in Davenport, and Mexicans in Bettendorf (long before the white middle class moved in), the latter recruited by the Bettendorf brothers to fill a labor shortage during World War I.

A couple of generations got a better standard of living thanks to those factories, but eventually most of them closed. Rather than getting stuck with aging industrial buildings along the riverfront, the cities of the region tore down most of those old plants and created a network of riverfront trails and parks. If you were a 19th century resident of Rock Island or Davenport, you'd have a hard time recognizing the 21st century version of your city, except for a few fragments here and there.

As I ran along the river, spotting those remnants was like flipping through pages of living history: elegant twin suspension bridges, the 19th century frame buildings in East Davenport, a stone pier left from the first railroad bridge across the Mississippi (a replica), a baseball stadium, casinos. These may all be pieces of local history, but each says something about the way our relationship to the river has changed over time, regardless of where we live. We no longer see the river as critical to the economic success of our cities (unless you are one of those shipping companies). Today we see the river mostly as a source of recreation, a place to swim or fish or something pretty to look at, maybe something to attract a few tourist dollars. But mostly we don't think much about it at all.

I had picked a warm day for my run—nearly 80 degrees, unusually warm for early April. The sun was getting low on the horizon and a breeze blew across the river, threatening to sweep away the day's warmth. I set out from the motel in Bettendorf and headed west toward East Davenport.

Most of the time when I run I get into a zone, I can forget about everything else going on in my world. Not on that day, though. Even as I pushed myself to run faster than normal, I couldn't get my mind to slow down, and I barely noticed anything around me. I kept thinking about Miguel, wondering if something I did contributed to his death, worrying about how I was going to clear my name without getting into all the details of exactly what happened that night. It would be better for everyone, especially for me, if some things didn't come out. I just didn't know how I was going to keep a lid on it all with the FBI, the Moline police, and a reporter all nosing around. If the case was somehow solved quickly, then what I did Friday night wouldn't matter to anyone, except me.

Before I realized it, I had passed by Bucktown—Davenport's infamous but extinct red light district—and I had reached the Centennial Bridge. I had already covered three miles, and I still had to backtrack. I lost steam around the five-mile mark and walked the last mile back to the motel. Before the Twin Bridges, I caught sight of a couple of guys fishing. When I got close, I recognized the stylized crucifix on the right arm of one of them.

"Small world, bumping into you here," I said to Noah, the bartender from the Crooked Spine.

He turned to look at me. "Hey, it's the travel writer. You found me at my favorite spot to fish. Don't put it in your book, OK? I don't want to share it with nobody."

"I promise. Catch anything?" I asked as he looked away to bait a hook.

"Nothing worth keeping. Hoping to get a catfish before the day's over."

"Do you eat what you catch here? I mean, aren't you worried at all about the pollution in the river?"

"Nah. I might if I ate river fish every day, but every

once in a while's fine. Besides, cut it into nuggets and fry it with a cornmeal batter, and it goes real well with one of my homemade pale ales."

"You brew your own beer?"

"Sure do. Don't care much for the popular beers; too watery for me. I like my beer to taste like something."

"I'm not a fan of those beers, either. Give me a full-bodied beer, like a good stout."

"As I recall, you had a porter the other night, a good choice."

"What do you brew?"

"I don't make a big variety, usually a nice hoppy IPA or a pale ale. I've got a barley wine aging right now; looking forward to that one for New Year's. Did you have any luck finding some music the other night?"

"I wouldn't call it music, but there was a singer-songwriter playing at Rolling Rapids. Didn't care much for it. My friend, Miguel, the guy I met at Crooked Spine, dragged me out of there before I had the chance to do the world a favor and break the guy's guitar."

"I hear he ran into some bad luck, Miguel, the Mexican." Noah turned away from me and cast a line in the water.

"If you consider getting murdered bad luck, then yeah. And he was born in Texas, by the way, which means he was an American."

"Whatever. I don't approve of knocking someone off, but I'm having a hard time working up sympathy for that guy. He had it coming."

"What do you mean?"

"My friends always tell me I need to learn when to

shut up, so maybe this is one of those times. I'll just say that there was something more than a little shady about that guy. Never trusted him."

"Did he do something to you directly? Like stealing from you or stiffing you on a tip?"

"No, not exactly like that." He reeled in his line and immediately cast it back out, never turning around to look at me. "Look, I've said enough already. I shouldn't speak ill of the dead."

"Right. Well, I need to finish this run, anyway, and get cleaned up. I'm glad I bumped into you. Good luck with your fishing."

"Take it easy, man. Watch your back."

Back at the room, I took a leisurely shower, wondering why Noah didn't warn me to watch my back a little sooner. He obviously wasn't a fan of Miguel, but I had a hard time imagining what Miguel could have done to him. Maybe Noah didn't like students. Or maybe he knew about Miguel's past troubles with the law. Or maybe Noah just had a problem with Mexicans.

I was about to lie down for a quick nap—a post-workout tradition—when my phone rang. It was Ruby, the grandmother I wished I'd had.

"Honey. How are you? I just talked with Madame Magenta." She calls the Madame, her personal psychic, once a week for readings and advice, whether she needs it or not. "She told me that there was a lot of bad energy around you right now, so I got worried. Is everything OK?"

Ruby Beck lives upriver in the small river town of Friesburg, Iowa, not far from Dubuque. We met a few years ago when she was working as a volunteer in the town's museum. She's barely five feet tall, but she looks more imposing after a visit to the salon when her hair rises high like a silo on the Great Plains. As she was guiding me around the museum, she stopped in front of a locked glass cabinet to point out two small porcelain figures. She singled out one item in particular that had been positioned with its back turned to face out. She opened the cabinet and pulled it out to show me that the piece depicted a female figure, breasts fully bared for all to appreciate. One of the volunteers, someone with an overdeveloped sense of modesty and the right key, had unlocked the bookcase and turned the figure to face toward the back so those bare breasts couldn't be appreciated by anyone. "I don't think that's right," Ruby said. "I think we should show things as they really are." That's when I knew the same blood ran in our veins.

After that, our conversations got more personal. I reminded her of her son, a man, who, by all accounts, was well-rounded and family-oriented, and smarter than most, with a passion for art and science. I was flattered that she saw all that in me, but I doubted that I really measured up. Every time I passed through Friesburg, which was often, we'd have lunch. I didn't know if Ruby's call was really prompted by the psychic's comments, but she always had a good sense of timing. Somehow she always knew when I needed a little encouragement.

"Life has been better," I told her. "I met a guy, a student at Dickey Chiropractic School, that I wanted to write about, but something happened to him. He was murdered early in the morning after we met. The police think I was the last person to talk to him, so they've made me a suspect in his death. Other than that, I'm fine."

"Well that's the most ridiculous thing I've ever heard. Those police must be really desperate or dumb. There's no way you could hurt someone, much less murder that boy. What are you going to do?"

"I'm trying to figure out what really happened. My friend, Brian Jefferson, the homicide cop from St. Louis I've told you about, came up here to help out. We're still puzzled by it all. We even got a personal visit from Agent Starck, from the FBI. I'm pretty sure he doesn't see me as a suspect, but it's hard to tell."

"I suppose that's good, to have one of them on your side, anyway. Did you say his name is Starck? That sounds familiar for some reason."

"Yeah. Starck."

"Is there anything I can do to help out?"

"Nah. I think we'll find a way to figure things out. So what's new in Friesburg?"

"Oh, don't get me started. That stupid city council is trying to close the museum again. They don't know what they're doing. They don't spend any money on advertising then they complain that no one ever visits it. Well, how can anyone visit a place that they don't even know exists?"

Ruby has been a volunteer at the museum since she retired. For over 25 years she has been studying the museum's trove of trinkets, antiques, and collectibles, getting to know it better than anyone, maybe even better than Steve and Ann Jones, the folks who collected all those items in the first place. But she refuses to share that knowledge with the people who run the museum. She's afraid they'll use the information to create a catalog for an auction house.

"So now it's my turn to ask. Is there anything I can do to help you?"

"No, I don't think so. I think as soon as the money runs out, they'll close it and sell everything." The Joneses left an endowment to fund the museum's operation but it has been getting dangerously low and no one in a position of influence was inclined to do anything about it. Ruby might be right. The political leaders in the town didn't seem to value the museum at all, but, because of the terms of the Joneses' will, they were powerless to do anything to liquidate its assets until the endowment was gone. Hearing about Friesburg's political intrigue was a nice distraction from my own predicament.

"Don't you worry about me, Frank. You have enough going on right now. I'm going to call Madame Magenta back for a new reading. Maybe she can help us figure out what really happened to that poor young man."

"Let me know if she comes up with anything. Take care, Ruby."

"I will. And let me know when you're going to be in Friesburg again. There's a new place that just opened up on the river. We can have lunch there the next time."

Between the run and the call from Ruby, I was feeling better, my head a little clearer. After we hung up, I nursed a shot of whiskey and felt like I could actually sleep for a few hours.

14

I woke with a start in the middle of the night, wet with sweat and my heart racing. I wasn't sure where I was at first. Someone had been chasing me, and I knew he wasn't looking to give me a pat on the back. I was running as fast as I could and could see the edge of a cliff just ahead. I had to go over that cliff or my pursuer would catch up. My legs were beginning to feel heavy, and I thought I might be slowing down, but I didn't dare look behind me, to see who was after me; I kept looking straight ahead. I got to the edge of the cliff ahead of my pursuer and didn't hesitate; I went right over. I don't remember falling or even hitting anything, but I was suddenly having trouble breathing and even though my legs were churning, I wasn't moving very fast. I spun my head around a couple of times before I realized I was underwater. As the pressure in my lungs grew more intense, I caught a glimpse of a couple of figures above me and pushed my body hard upward toward them. When I burst through the surface, I saw two bodies floating lifeless on the surface, both face down with their arms extended to the side. I moved toward them slowly, kicking with my feet. As I got close, I recognized one of the bodies; it was Miguel, still wearing his Jaguars jacket, and not looking so good, his face was bleached and bloated. As I swam near him, I bumped into the other body, one much smaller than his. It swung around toward me, and the head popped up just enough for me to see a face I hadn't seen in a long time. I stared right into the vacant eyes of my sister, Tina. That's when I woke up. At least there was no rhino this time. I got up and splashed water on my face, staring in the mirror, rubbing my eyes. I went back to bed, but, for the rest of the night, I was in and out of sleep, always waking up just a few minutes short of dreaming again.

I might have managed a couple more hours of good sleep, but everyone in the motel showered and left at the same time; the pillow over my head was no match for the squealing pipes and the slamming doors. I put on a pot of coffee, the four-cup squat pot that comes standard in most motel rooms, but I cut the water in half to brew a cup that was dark and bitter, like my mood. Sitting at the desk, I flipped open my laptop and immediately looked up the *Moline Herald* website, where I found a news brief about a body that was found in Suiter Slough:

> *Moline police are investigating the death of a man whose body was pulled from Suiter Slough on Saturday morning. A man who went to the slough to fish spotted the body floating several feet from shore. Police know the identity of the victim but won't release his name until relatives are notified. Police consider the death suspicious; an autopsy will be conducted to determine the cause of death.*

I checked a couple of other news sources, as well, and saw the same thing. That's a relief. I don't mind keeping my name out of the press, at least when it's linked to a corpse.

Before I could check my email, Jefferson knocked on my door.

"You disappeared yesterday afternoon," I said, raising a hand to shield my eyes from the light. "Come in."

"It took a while to track people down, still trying to reach Starck, in fact, but I learned a few things. I found out a little more about this Cody guy. His name is Cody Hahn. He's also a student at Dickey but not a very good one. He's passing his classes, but barely. He's from Rock Island, grew up there. The Moline cops have already interviewed him. He doesn't remember much about that night, except for seeing you at the Crooked Spine. He remembered your hat."

I have a twenty-year-old fedora that I wear when I go out. It tends to get me noticed. "I knew that hat was going to be trouble some day."

"You do like being noticed, Frank. Cody told the cops that he thinks you killed Miguel, that you have a bad temper and probably lost your cool and knocked him in the water. I wouldn't worry about it, though. The cops don't believe much of what he's said so far."

"He and I never really hit it off."

"I guess not. Cody and Miguel shared an apartment, but the landlord said all the rent checks came from Miguel. Maybe Cody was slipping some cash to Miguel, but it looks like he may have been staying there rent-free."

"So other than being roommates, how did they know each other?" I asked.

"I don't know, yet. I only found out some of what he told the Moline cops. But I did find out that Cody had a couple thousand dollars, or more, deposited in his checking account every month since last October. The boy didn't work, Frank, and his parents are barely middle class. I don't think they're the kind of people who can drop two Gs in their son's bank account every month."

"So where was the money coming from?"

"Good question."

"Looks like you have some more asking around to do."

"Yeah. So let's get back to your night out with Miguel. What happened after you left that German place?" I made another pot of coffee, filling it up this time.

"We left the Schnitzel Haus and walked around the corner to the Rolling Rapids Brewpub. I love that place—really good beer, decent food, cheap."

"Sounds like your kind of place," Jefferson said.

"You know me. We found a couple of empty stools at the far end of the bar; the place was busy but not crowded. While we were waiting to get the attention of a bartender—the service at Rolling Rapids is slower than a stoned turtle—I steered the conversation back to Looney. I didn't want to seem too eager to hear about it but I didn't want to let an opportunity slip away, either. So I asked him a little more."

****

"You said John Looney was your grandfather, right?"

"Yeah," Miguel replied.

"So does that make you Irish-Mexican American?"

"I guess it does. Juan go bragh! Seriously, my family doesn't like to talk about the Irish side, but I'm not ashamed. We're mostly Mexican American, but my grandfather met my grandmother when she worked for his family in New Mexico. I think she was their housekeeper. They got pretty tight, I guess, and had a baby, my dad. They weren't married, so people were all hush-hush about it. My dad told me the story, but he made me promise not to bring it up at family reunions. He said it was hard enough to see those relatives and know they looked down on him; he didn't need them saying nasty things to his face, too." Miguel smiled. "Dad couldn't help mix in some bullshit when he was telling me something; I never had to worry about outing our secret, because we never went to any family reunions, none that I remember."

One of the bartenders finally noticed us and ambled down in our direction, past the row of copper brewing kettles, the ten taps, and about a dozen confused looks from other people who were wondering when a bartender would notice that they were thirsty, too. With a coffee stout and a honey lager on the way, I went back to quizzing Miguel.

"So what did your father tell you about Looney?"

"That he was some kind of big-time gangster. He was the man who controlled the bars and the booze and the girls and the games. People were afraid of him and shit, but he always looked out for his family. Family first, you know. I think he even did some time, in prison, you know, but I don't know what they got him for. That's what I learned about my granddad."

****

110

"Sounds like Miguel had a crush on his grandfather," Jefferson said.

I chuckled. "You could be right, Brian. But Miguel wasn't entirely wrong, you know. Besides the newspaper, Looney controlled the distribution of booze during the early days of Prohibition, brothels, gambling, and dozens of bars. He also made a lot of money from stealing cars, as you know, and selling them all across the US."

"I know, I know, professor; he had a diversified business portfolio, as you've said over and over, and wrote in that best-selling book of yours."

"No need to get insulting. I brought a copy of that book along, thinking that I would give it to Miguel at some point."

"Sorry, brother. I know how proud you were of it."

"Are. I'm still proud of it."

"Of course you are."

"After Miguel told me his fantasy version of Looney, I got to thinking about how Looney used the liquor trade and his bars to regain control of the vice scene in Rock Island after he came back. How did that work, again?" I picked up *Too Looney for the Law* and started flipping through the pages. "Let's see; I think it was in chapter 4. Here it is," I began, without looking at Jefferson.

> The Tri-Cities, as the area was known then, was rife with corruption, and the vice trade was easy money. Davenport's Bucktown district was known across the US for its gambling halls and general lawlessness. Characters like Brick Munro ran burlesque theaters and bars like The Senator and The Ozark that were infamous for their high-stakes

poker tables. Bucktown had a legion of young ladies who catered to the physical needs of the gamblers, drinkers, and musicians. Bare-knuckle fights were staged for hundreds of spectators (and usually rigged).

Music was an integral part of the scene. A young Al Jolson worked as a waiter in one of the clubs, singing for beer and tips. Black musicians from Memphis and St. Louis made regular stops; Bucktown was one of the few white-dominated districts where they were allowed to play. Looney was eager to get in on the action and would eventually control access to all the popular vices in Rock Island and extend his influence up and down the Mississippi River.

Looney slowly emerged from exile in 1919, reestablishing control of the underground economy in Rock Island in a remarkably short period of time. By 1920 he was once again the criminal kingpin in the Quad Cities. Old allies—Dan Drost and Anthony Billburg—became enemies. Former enemies, like Harry Schriver, the mayor who nearly killed Looney in 1912, were now allies.

Looney's bars never closed; they didn't even have locks on the doors, didn't need them. While police in other cities sometimes raided speakeasies, if only for show, the Rock Island cops didn't even bother with a dress rehearsal. An undercover journalist for the *Argus* found that gin and whiskey were popular during Prohibition and were often served in plain sight of the cops, if not directly to the cops. Everyone was making money, especially Looney, who had a number of creative ways to raise cash, like requiring the bars he supplied with booze to purchase ads in his newspaper, the *News*.

Helen Van Dale (born Catherine Helena Lee) ran the prostitution business for Looney, which was reputedly the largest in the country at that time. Girls from across the US came to Rock Island to work the brothels. Van Dale sent many of them to other places to work, like to Johnny Torrio's clubs in Chicago. Some of Looney's most exclusive brothels catered to white guys who favored a darker-skinned gal. Besides those black women, Looney also had an express service that brought girls up from Mexico. Maybe he liked the darker-skinned girls, too. For the most part, Looney ran a tight ship, making plenty of money for himself and for all the right people. If someone got out of line, Looney took care of that, too. In 1922 alone, Rock Island recorded twelve murders and three suicides. John Looney was probably responsible for all of them.

"So, yeah, Miguel's understanding of his grandfather's business was rather limited. You can stop pacing now, Brian."

"Is story-telling time over?"

"For now. So what do you think about the way Miguel looked up to Looney? I'm a little confused by it, honestly. Maybe after a couple of generations, the murder and mayhem seem cute. We idolize a lot of gangsters after they die: Jesse James, Al Capone, Bonnie and Clyde; the list isn't a short one. I think those characters appeal to the outlaw in all of us: Fuck authority! Fuck the man! Fuck the harm they caused! Even cops are even guilty of romanticizing some of those old-school gangsters, I bet."

"I can't speak for every cop out there, Frank, but, yeah, I love that gangster history. You know that. Those were classic battles, cops versus gangsters, gangsters against gangsters. I admit it—I admire the way they took care of their own and didn't take shit from anyone. It wasn't like they were a bunch of big thinkers trying to change the world. They were just businessmen looking out for their interests, by any means necessary. The shit we deal with today is different; it's a war that goes on and on, but for no good reason. Those gangsters, they were men. Today we have kids shooting at us. Ain't nothing romantic about that."

"Just businessmen, huh? Even after all these years of knowing you, you still throw a few surprises at me. So I was about to tell Miguel about the real legacy of his grandfather, all the people who died, the lives he ruined, how he stole money from his own mother, but the musician finally got started at Rolling Rapids, and I had a hard time hearing what Miguel was saying. We stopped to listen for a while, and Miguel used the break in our conversation to send out a few more text messages."

****

The singer had set up across the room from us, introduced himself as Rain-Dance—probably not his birth name. He was from Minneapolis and called himself a singer-songwriter and folk-rocker. I guess you can be

114

both. He bragged that he wasn't into classroom learning, that he was a self-taught guitar player. Judging by the way he played, he wasn't much into pitch or key, either. His first song was a cover of Neil Young's Heart of Gold. By the time he got into Helpless, I thought he was reading my mind. When he started singing Old Man, my life flashed before my eyes.

"I'm getting prematurely old listening to this fucking crap," I said as I leaned into Miguel, who turned to look at me, not sure what to say.

Old man look at my life, I'm a lot like you were...

"Doesn't he have any songs of his own to butcher? I mean, if he had a tin ear, that would be an improvement. He's not tone deaf, he's tone indifferent." I nearly yelled that last insult. I was getting restless. I've heard a lot of bad music in my day and don't have the patience left to waste my remaining years sitting through more of it.

"Dude, calm down. He's not so bad. He's really trying." Miguel fidgeted and looked around at the people near us.

Doesn't mean that much to me, To mean that much to you.

I took a deep breath, hoping to get in touch with the part of me that can tolerate anything, but instead I drilled into a reservoir of resentment. "He sucks, man, and you know it. I'm so sick of these hacks getting an audience in places like this. Doesn't anyone screen the acts they book? Or do they just book any fucker with a guitar and a Neil Young playlist?"

Miguel leaned away from me and looked around the

bar. "This place got busy, huh?" he said.

I stood up and yelled: "You should fire your guitar teacher. And your voice coach, too!" Rain-Dance stopped playing and looked at me; he looked confused and hurt, but willing to forgive. A few people sitting near us told me to shut up and sit down, although I also got a few subtle thumbs up and winks.

That was enough for Miguel, though. "So let's get the fuck out of here if you hate it so much." He grabbed my arm and pulled me to the door.

I was relieved to be outside.

"Man, what was that about? He wasn't that bad," Miguel said.

"Yes, he was that bad. I hate that shit. He was just one bad musician too far." Miguel stood with his arms crossed, staring me down. "I'm sorry. I didn't mean to get so worked up. And to get you so worked up. Sorry." I tried to look remorseful, even if I wasn't sincere. "You up for one more place or are you sick of me, yet? I promise I'll behave."

Miguel gave me a good look-over, trying to figure out if I was unstable or just drunk, I suppose. "You ever been to the Locked Down? It's back in Davenport."

"No. Sounds like fun. Let's go."

As we walked back to the car, I turned to him and said "Your grandpa was an asshole, you know."

"What do you mean?"

"He was a thief, a murderer, a liar, and he stole from his own mother. But I'm sure he helped a few old ladies across the street, too."

15

My phone rang before I could tell Jefferson what happened next. "Let me see who this is, Brian."

"Frank? Is that you?"

The voice on the other end of the phone, familiar and unwelcome, was tightly-controlled; the pitch had less range than cattle in a feedlot. Jackie Spear was one of the PhDs that ran the practice I fled a few years ago. She was less toxic than some of the other partners—more like E. coli than Ebola—but I wouldn't exactly call her warm. I had no idea why she would be calling me, but it probably wasn't a good sign.

"Frank. I hate to be the one to tell you this, but I have bad news. Your old colleague, Anna Hanks, passed away last night."

I was sure she didn't hate telling me the news. If she had a real specialty as a psychologist, it was as the person who couldn't wait to deliver bad news.

"I just found out from a friend and thought you might not hear from anyone else. You're out of town so often. I wasn't sure if you even knew that she'd been diagnosed with stomach cancer. That was just two months ago. I'm so sorry, Frank. You must be devastated. I haven't heard from you for a while. I hope you are doing OK, you know, since you ran away from everyone here."

"That's sweet of you to be concerned. I'm doing

117

fine. Never happier. Thanks again for passing along the news about Anna. I'll take it from here. All my best to the crew."

I hung up and sat down. Anna Hanks was dead. Jackie was right: I didn't know that Anna had cancer. I needed to call her family and find out what's going on, if they needed anything, even if I couldn't get away right now to talk to them in person. Hanks was about twenty years older than me, somewhere between a mother and a big sister. She had entered my life so effortlessly that I couldn't imagine a time when she wasn't a part of it.

I met her when I started graduate school. I wouldn't have finished the Master's program without her support and her ability to administer a well-timed kick in the ass when I was standing still too long. After I graduated, she became a trusted confidante as I entered the world of professional practice. She'd been there. She knew the pitfalls and the games and the damaged people that could make my life miserable—colleagues, mostly. I wouldn't have lasted as long as I did without her support.

Hanks wasn't always the most popular person on the faculty, in fact, she engaged in outright war with a couple of them for reasons that probably spoke more to her stubbornness than her principles. Some students found her rigid and narrow minded, but I never had that problem with her. It's true that some of her views of the world and about people were a bit...dated. But, in her heart, fairness and justice trumped whatever stereotypes lingered in her mind and, over time, she became more open to people with different ways of viewing the world and different experiences.

We kept in touch, even after I left my therapist job to travel around the world. While our communiqués became less frequent, they were never shallow. We kept up by email most of the time, but when I was back home in St. Louis we always found time for lunch. The last time was nine months ago when I passed through for a few days. She never gave me a hard time about turning my life upside down, although I know she was puzzled by it. If she had been in the same position, felt what I was feeling, I think she would have held steady, looking to her family and friends to balance out the bullshit at work. But that's not who I am, and she knew it. Even if the direction I chose confounded her, she helped me come up with story ideas and sent me names of publications she thought I should write for. I'd miss her.

I dealt with a lot of clients over the years who had a hard time moving on after losing someone they loved. They all experienced grief in different ways; some I admired and some I abhorred, but I usually found something clinical to say. I have had a hard time figuring out how to comfort friends, though, who've lost someone close to them. Maybe I put too much pressure on myself to say the right thing. When it happens to me, after all, when I lose someone important, I'm not consoled by words. In the next few days, someone might say something like "She may not be here physically, but you'll always have your memories of her." I'm sorry, but I don't find that comforting. I have good memories of a lobster dinner I ate in Maine, but I'd find eating another lobster much more satisfying than the memory of one.

With Hanks' death, I had lost two friends, one new

and one old, in three days. I'm not superstitious, but I couldn't shake the belief that bad things happen in threes.

"Frank. What's up?" I almost forgot that Jefferson was in the room with me.

"My adviser from grad school just passed. I gotta check with her family and see what's going on."

"I'm sorry, Frank. That's terrible. I hate to say this, but you know you're probably stuck up here for a while. I don't know if it's a good idea to leave right now, even for a funeral."

I turned away, quickly wiping my eyes. I knew he was right, but I still didn't like it. Living on the road, I was accustomed to missing out on a lot of things. I rarely make it to weddings, which is fine by me. I hate weddings. I'm not around for the drama when Jack and Jill or Jack and Steve split up. I miss most CD release parties and baptisms and soft openings and happy hours; I usually find out who won the World Series or Super Bowl long after the games were played. But I don't miss funerals; I hate missing funerals, especially this one.

"I know. I know," I sighed. "Give me a little time right now, though. I gotta check with her family."

"Alright. I'll go back to my room. I should call my wife, anyway, I suppose," Jefferson said on the way out the door.

I didn't get to talk directly to Hanks' husband, which I expected. He had a lot going on. I talked with Hanks' brother instead, who gave me the scoop on the plans for a memorial service on Friday. I told him I hoped to be there but work might get in the way. He didn't need to know the details. The family was still in shock. Hanks' death had happened so quickly that no one had time to prepare to grieve.

After I got off the phone, Jefferson came shooting back over to my room.

"Cody was blackmailing Ramirez."

16

"I thought you were going to call Michelle," I said.

"Yeah, I meant to but I decided I needed to check in again with my contact at the police department, in case he had any news."

Jefferson's contact in the Moline Police Department—some guy he went to the academy with—had been sharing details about what the investigation had turned up so far. The police had been digging into the life of Cody Hahn, who, it turned out, had a few secrets. While he had looks that rivaled Adonis and abundant confidence, he did poorly in school and had trouble holding down a job. He was lucky to get into the Dickey College of Chiropractic. Stuck on the waiting list for a few weeks, he was admitted just before the new term began when a couple of students decided to go elsewhere . His college grades were barely passable, but he had good letters of recommendation and that was just enough to get him in. He was also a local boy, growing up across the river in Rock Island, which might have helped; Dickey was known to bend the rules to help local students. Miguel was initially assigned a different roommate, but he changed his mind about going to Dickey, so Miguel got Cody as a last-minute replacement. That's how they met.

While Jefferson and I had spent years speculating about whether Looney had any descendants, Miguel was telling anyone who would listen that his grandfather was John Looney. It didn't register with a lot of people, though, who assumed a gangster named Looney had to be a comic book character. But Cody was from Rock Island and, while he ignored a lot of what was taught in school, the stories about Looney got his attention. He remembered those.

"So he was blackmailing Miguel for being related to a gangster?" I asked.

"That's what I thought at first, which didn't really make sense. No, there's more. Miguel had his own legal troubles. Seems he got in pretty deep running drugs, and not just for some neighborhood hoodlums; he got caught running drugs across the US-Mexico border, at least that's what Cody said."

"How did Cody find that out?"

"They were out drinking, got stinking drunk, and Miguel told him that he'd been arrested for drug trafficking when he was in college. Said he was trying to pay off some debts, but then he got caught, and he's never stopped paying since."

"So Cody claims Miguel was a drug runner? How did that go over with the cops?"

"They don't know what to think, yet, but they aren't convinced. They haven't been able to find any records of Miguel being arrested or charged with anything, much less for a drug-related offense."

"Huh. Between the blackmailing and that mysterious monthly deposit in his bank account, Cody doesn't look very good, does he?" That was the best news I'd had since this whole investigation began. I couldn't help but feel a little delight in the fact that Cody, that smug little twit, was looking like a prime suspect.

"Yeah, Cody's in the crosshairs right now but don't get too excited. He could be making shit up to cover his ass for some other reason. Maybe he's prepping for some kind of self-defense claim. You know, behind Miguel's nice-guy appearance was a dangerous drug dealer who tried to kill him on Friday night, so naturally Cody had to respond."

"Maybe."

I hadn't told Jefferson, yet, but I already knew about Miguel's past troubles with the law. Cody wasn't lying.

"What about the FBI? We know that they had been watching him for some reason. This has to be why, right?"

"I'm checking on that. I haven't been able to corner Agent Starck, yet, but I'm still working on it. But enough of that for now. I don't want you to get distracted by what the cops are doing right now. I want to hear the rest of the story about your night running with Miguel. You left Rolling Rapids and were headed to the Locked Down, and you had just called his grandfather a punk."

"Right," I said. "Miguel wasn't thrilled with me after I yelled at Rain-Dance but, after I made those comments about Looney, he was really pissed off. He confronted me when we got to the car."

****

"What do you fucking mean he stole from his mother?" He pushed me on the shoulder, forcing me against the car. "That's fucked up. I mean, I could see that he had people killed. He was a fucking gangster, OK? But you're making up that shit about his mother. And how do you know about him, anyway?"

He turned around and stepped away from me. I leaned away from the car and approached him, putting my hand on his shoulder when I got near. "It's my business to know. Remember? I write about the history of places along the Mississippi, like Rock Island." Miguel shrugged off my touch and took another step away from me. "Look. I don't want to be mean, but you have no idea who your grandfather really was. He wasn't some romantic Robin Hood-type figure who stole from the greedy to give to the needy. He was an immoral crook, a selfish, ruthless killer who did whatever he had to do to make a buck. He exploited everyone, even those who were close to him, especially those who were close to him." I stepped toward Miguel, keeping my hands to myself this time. "He controlled his mother's finances the last few years of her life and bilked every penny he could from her estate; while he lived in mansions, she died penniless in a convent. Looney dragged his only son, Connor, into the family business, and it didn't end well; Connor bled to death in the middle of 17th Street, shot to death in a gun fight; he was 22. Looney never felt a need to confess to ripping off his own mother and never shed a tear over the loss of his son." I didn't actually know if Looney felt remorse about his mother or grief over the loss of his son, but I was trying to make a point.

Miguel finally turned around to face me. "I didn't know those things. No one told me those stories." He dropped his head, unable to maintain eye contact with me. "I wish they had. I heard so many stories from my dad about Looney; I figured that's who he wanted me to be, who my dad was trying to be. I feel like I've been trying to live up to the family reputation since I was a kid. I tried so hard to be bad like my dad and granddad, that I got myself in trouble."

"What do you mean?"

"I don't really want to get into it, but I did some shit I'm not proud of. And I got caught. The thing is, I did it because I felt like I was expected to do it, to get involved in gambling and drugs and shit. But it never felt right to me. It wasn't me."

"And I guess you weren't so good at it if you got caught," I said. He didn't smile. "At least it's all in the past now, right?"

"If only," he said, as we got in the car. Miguel stared ahead vacantly for a few seconds, then he turned to face me, eyes narrowing. "I feel like I've been doing all the talking tonight. So what's your story, really?"

"What do you mean?"

"I don't know, man. You said you're a writer, so you must be a pretty good one. You've dropped some cash tonight on food and drinks. You're on the road a lot. So you make a good living, right?"

"No, I really don't, by most people's standards." I started the engine and pulled out, driving toward Davenport.

"So you must have some other way of making money, huh? I mean, a guy's gotta do what he's gotta do to stay afloat, right?"

"I suppose." I didn't know what he was getting at.

"The thing is, Miguel, I don't make a lot of money, but I live cheaply. I don't owe anyone a dime. Like I told you, I was a therapist for a long time before I started writing, so I managed to save some money. That's come in handy the past few years, that's for sure."

"Still, being on the road a lot, you meet a lot of people, make a lot of contacts. That must come in handy."

"Sure. I know a lot of people along the river. I don't make a lot of money, but I never lack for company." That seemed to mollify him, either that or the sight of the Locked Down Tavern did.

I squeezed my car in between two Dodge pickups, and we went inside. That's when we saw Cody again.

"Shit. I'm really not in the mood for him right now."

17

The Locked Down Tavern is an old corner bar on the east side of downtown Davenport, an area that, like many of its customers, peaked during the Cold War. It's within spitting distance of the Mississippi River and downriver from the dam that tamed the Rock Island Rapids. Standing out front, you can watch towboats pushing barges through the lock and the old government bridge swing open to let the boats pass by. Who you meet at the bar depends on when you're there. The happy hour crowd is mostly blue collar employees of the arsenal, guys who build small arms for the US government at the military installation on a nearby island. By 10pm, the bar is full of a mix of professionals and amateurs—alcoholics who went right from breast milk to moonshine and college students just getting started, both groups drawn by the cheap drinks and fleeting relationships.

"That was the first time you ran into Cody since the night began, right?" Jefferson asked.

"Yeah. Miguel wasn't thrilled to see him and didn't try to hide his feelings. His mumbled a few insults and his face turned red; he looked like he was steeling himself to do battle. That's when I learned a little more about Cody."

****

"Who is this guy?" I asked Miguel.

"My roommate."

"I guess you have issues."

Cody saw us before we had a chance to turn around and find another place for a drink. He waved at us, or at Miguel anyway, to come over to the bar. "Hey, bitch," he slurred. "Where've you been? I thought it was supposed to be you and me tonight?"

"Sorry. We lost track of time."

"Who is this dude anyway? Why are you hanging with him instead of me? You're supposed to be looking out for me tonight, remember bitch?"

Miguel didn't flinch. "Take it easy, man. He's a writer, Frank. He travels all over the world, and he's pretty cool, even though he can be really fucking rude." Miguel looked in my direction as he added that last part.

"And you are…" I asked as I reached my hand out to shake his. No response. He didn't even look at me.

"Shit. Be nice, man," said Miguel. He turned to me and said, "That's Cody, my roommate."

"Nice to meet you, Cody," I said, still unable to get a response.

Cody fixed his gaze on Miguel but didn't say a word. Miguel didn't back down, maintaining eye contact before finally breaking the silence. "We've been having a crazy night. We learned a German drinking song, at least part of one, from real fucking Germans. What did you do tonight?" I think Miguel already knew the answer to that one.

"I want a drink," Cody responded. "You got this one, Miguelito?"

"Let me," I jumped in. I hoped that, if I bought a round, Cody would calm down, so I could get back to talking to Miguel.

"What do you want?" I asked. Cody finally looked in my direction, but he just glared at me.

"A shot of Jameson and a Stag," Cody answered, then he turned back at Miguel.

"And you?" I asked Miguel.

"Just a Stag. Thanks." At least Miguel said thanks.

I went to the bar and ordered two shots of Jameson and three Stags, while Cody and Miguel drifted toward a corner. I couldn't hear what they were saying, but their voices got louder and louder, and I was pretty sure that the only thing that stopped Cody from punching Miguel was my timely reappearance, with drinks in hand.

Cody shot the Jameson and the Stag, then excused himself to use the bathroom.

I downed my shot of whiskey, then suggested that we step outside. "I could use a smoke," I said.

"Let's go. I didn't know you smoked."

"I don't." We went out to the patio, a concrete pad with a privacy fence around it and tiki torches in the corners, and I bummed a cigarette from a young woman who was half a beer from passing out. She had a pack of American Spirits. American Spirits: they're all natural! At least that's how I used to rationalize it back when I smoked them every day. I'm just about the worst kind of smoker now: only when I drink, and only if someone else paid for it.

"So what's going on?" I asked Miguel.

"We have a complicated relationship."

I took a deep drag, letting the smoke caress my throat and lungs before I exhaled a pale cloud away from Miguel. "Tell me about it. Maybe I can help."

"I just wish I hadn't told him about my past, you know? Like I told you, I did some dumb shit, like really dumb. And I got caught."

"And you told Cody about it?"

"I wasn't planning on it. I had just moved here and didn't know anyone, so I was real glad to get a roommate who seemed like a cool guy. We got along pretty good, too, at least in the beginning. One night we were out at the bars, and I had way too much to drink. I just blurted out that I got busted a while ago for bringing drugs to the US from Mexico."

"Shit, Miguel. Bringing drugs across the border? That's not some minor offense."

"I know; believe me, I know. It's a long story, but I shouldn't have told Cody any of it."

"How did he react?" I asked.

"He started calling me gangster and shit like that."

I chuckled. Miguel didn't. "Sorry. I'm not making fun of you. I'm laughing at Cody. He sounds like someone who grew up in a ranch house on a cul-de-sac listening to hip hop and wearing his baseball cap backwards at school, figuring that's what it meant to be tough." Miguel grinned. "You said you got caught, but you're here now, so that's a good sign, right?"

"I had to make a deal to turn in some other guys. That's another reason I came up here for school. It wasn't a good idea for me to stay in south Texas much longer."

"I suppose when you turn someone in, they and their

friends aren't too happy with you."

"That's an understatement."

****

"Fine," Jefferson interrupted, walking over to the sink to pour a glass of water. "So you already knew he'd been in trouble. I guess Cody wasn't making that part up. I wonder why the Moline police haven't been able to verify it?" Jefferson asked, mostly to himself. "I suppose if he cut a deal before any charges were filed, there wouldn't be anything on his record, but you'd think the FBI might say something about it to the Moline cops."

"So where does that leave us? What do we do next?"

"First, you're gonna finish telling me about the rest of your night, then I'm going to try a little harder to get in contact with that Agent Starck."

18

After I finished the cigarette on the patio, Miguel and I wandered back inside the Locked Down. Cody was sitting at the bar but every stool near him was empty. He didn't look very stable; I could see his head moving around, like a worn out bobblehead doll. He was stinking drunk when we got there, so whatever self control he had left when we arrived was swept away by the additional beer and whiskey.

Cody flopped his head around enough to notice that we were back in the bar. He stumbled in our direction, but before he could say anything, Miguel turned to me, "Hey, the pool table just opened up. Do you play?"

"Sure. Let's give it a shot." We walked into the next room; Cody trailed along behind us, following a less direct path, not saying a word.

Miguel set up the first rack. I'm a decent pool player, but not usually good enough to beat strangers who hang around pool tables in bars. I don't ever play them for money, though I've been known to buy a round or two after losing. Cody leaned against the far wall, and set down a can of Stag on top of a cigarette machine, or at least he thought he did. The can fell to the floor, spilling all over the worn vinyl tiles. Miguel glanced over at him.

"You should go home, man."

"Thank you very much, but I'm not ready to go

home. I'm just now having a good time."

Cody picked up the can, wiped off its mouth with the bottom of his Snoop Dog t-shirt, and drank what was left. The floor tiles actually looked a little cleaner, even though no one had mopped up the beer.

"See? I'm fine," he said. "Continue." He waved us on with a flick of his hand.

Miguel and I took turns missing shots. Every now and then Cody would say something like "I could take both of you bitches," but we ignored him. I finally sank a couple in a row and teased Miguel about it. For a few minutes, we almost forgot that Cody was there.

"About fucking time," Cody called out, reminding us that he was there.

As our game dragged on, Miguel and I didn't say much to each other, but every now and then, after another ball bounced around and out of a pocket, I caught his eye and realized that we were in a holding pattern, trying to prolong the game enough for Cody to pass out or lose interest or just disappear. It wasn't working, though. The guy had stamina.

"You guys suck," he yelled. "You're a sorry excuse for a gangster." I think that was meant for Miguel, who didn't take it well.

"I'm not a gangster, man," Miguel erupted, looking around the room to see who might have heard. "Stop calling me that. You don't know what you're talking about."

Cody wasn't going to stop. "Gangster, gangster. Bitch of Mexican drug lords. Get your cocaine here!" Each sentence a little louder than the last.

"Shut up, man!" Miguel moved toward Cody.

"Mule, mule. Cram drugs up your ass and cross the border," he sang, then turned around, bent over, and patted his butt.

I was losing patience, too. I moved around the other side of the pool table, underneath the neon Old Style sign, and got to Cody before Miguel did. "It's time for you to get out of here," I said, staring him down as I grabbed his arm. "I'll call you a cab."

"Don't bother, motha fucka. Let go of me. Miguel's supposed to have my back; he'll take care of me tonight. Won't you Miguelito?"

"I don't think Miguel's in the mood for this tonight. Just go home and sleep it off."

"Yeah, bro. Just go home. We'll get you a taxi," Miguel added.

I should have known better than to try to talk sense to someone who drowned his own hours earlier.

"Why you on his side?" Cody yelled out as he turned to face Miguel. "You're supposed to have my back. I suppose you're gonna snitch on me next."

"You don't know what you're talking about. Go home."

"Like I'm gonna leave you with some dude you just met. What do you really know about him? He's a writer? Fuck that. You just met him. You have to pick me over him. Have to."

"Go home," Miguel yelled as he turned and walked away.

Cody swiveled in my direction. "And what about you, dude? What's in it for you?"

If Rain-Dance the singer-songwriter wore thin on my nerves, Cody the angry drunk was rubbing them raw. I was ready to be rid of him; he was keeping me from digging into Miguel's story.

"Go home. You're done here, punk," I said, as I got in his face, showering his forehead with bits of spittle from an over-articulated 'p.'

"I don't know what your game is, dude, but I know your type. You're hiding something. What are you really after, pops?" He saw my wager of spittle and raised me two spits.

"I don't answer to you, you little fucker. I know your type, too—chronic drunk, parasite, pissed when you aren't the center of attention. Look, I'm giving you an easy out. I'll pay for a cab so you can get your sorry ass home in one piece."

"Fuck off," he yelled, trying to push me away or punch me, but just knocking off my glasses and hat while missing the rest of my body.

Turning to Miguel, he yelled, "I can out you, you know. I know your secrets."

"I know yours, too," Miguel countered. "I have just as much dirt on you. You should be paying me to shut up."

"It's not the same, dude. If I talk, you can kiss your chiropracty career good-bye and take your snitching ass back down to that crooked family of yours in Texas."

I was losing patience quickly. I took a couple of steps toward Cody, fists clenched and ready to punch him. But I held back.

"Back off, dude. You think I'm scared of some fucking writer? What are you going to do, explode a pen in my pocket? Besides, what you write about is shit," he yelled, placing a hand against the wall for balance. "The Mississippi is a fucking stink-hole of a sewer and the towns along the river are rotting, rat-infested ghost towns. You're a dumb-shit if you think anyone wants to read about that. I hope you fucking drown in it."

I couldn't resist any more after that. I punched him. I didn't think twice about it. I hit him in the gut, and when he hunched over, I put him on the floor with a right up-percut. It worked, sort of. He was out, but, unfortunately, the sight of him sprawled out on the floor, unconscious, bothered Miguel and made him feel responsible.

****

"You punched him? Seriously?" Jefferson asked.

"Yeah. I really did."

"If you'd fought like that when we were younger, you wouldn't have needed my protection." Jefferson thought it was hilarious that I hit someone, but I wasn't trying to be funny.

"Back to the story," I insisted. "Miguel wasn't too happy with the turn of events."

****

"Shit. I wish you didn't do that," he said. "I can't leave him there. I've gotta get him home."

"Damn. I'm really sorry about that. I'm short on pa-tience tonight. Let me help."

"Don't worry about it. He's my responsibility. I'll get

him back. You can call a taxi for me, though."

"Done."

"What are you going to do now?" Miguel asked.

"I'm not sure. I'm not ready to call it a night. I may run over to a casino for a while, maybe the Blackhawk, since that's about all there is to do this time of night."

"How long you gonna be in town?"

"I paid for a week at the motel where I'm staying, so I'll be here at least that long."

"Let me give you my number. We can hang out again before you go. Maybe tomorrow?"

"Sounds good to me."

I called a taxi for them. By the time it arrived, Cody was starting to come around, so I helped Miguel drag him into the back seat. And then they left. I walked over to the bar to apologize for punching a customer, but the bartender smiled and handed me another beer. "We hate that guy," she told me. "Every time he comes in here, he pisses someone off. You just did what a lot of people in here have been wanting to do."

****

"After I finished the beer, I drove to the casino," I told Jefferson. "I didn't expect to hear from Miguel again that night."

"But you did," Jefferson said. "He sent you that text message later."

"Yeah, he did," I said as I looked down. "But that wasn't the last time I saw him alive, either."

19

"Frank, are you telling me you saw him alive after he left the Locked Down? You told me he only sent you a text."

"Yeah. That wasn't entirely true." I paused. "OK; it's not true at all."

Before I could explain, my phone rang. "Let me get this," I said to Jefferson.

"Hi, Ruby. How are you?' I could see Jefferson glaring at me as I talked to Ruby. I walked toward the front window of the motel room, to put a little space between me and Jefferson.

"Oh, don't worry about me. How are you doing?" Ruby asked.

"I'm OK,"I said, watching Jefferson pace from one corner of the room to the other.

"Is there any more news about the investigation? I saw the paper printed a notice about the body that was found in Suiter Slough. How tragic. Such a waste of a life."

"Yeah; it's awful."

"Frank, I was thinking about something you said. You mentioned that you talked to a policeman named Starck?"

"Yeah; the FBI agent I talked to is named Starck. Why?"

"I thought that was the name. I remember hearing

139

about a policeman from Moline who got in trouble a few years ago. He killed a man who was accused of molesting young children, I think. It was all over the news for weeks. I think his name was Starck, too. Do you suppose they could be related?"

"I have no idea, but it doesn't seem like a very common name, does it? How long ago did that happen?"

"Oh, I'm not sure; maybe ten years ago? I can go to the library and try to find a newspaper story about it, if you think that would help."

"Sure. It couldn't hurt. It gives me a conversation starter the next time I see him, too. Thanks, Ruby."

"OK. I'll let you know what I find. Don't you worry, Frank. I'm sure everything will be fine. When do you think you'll be in Friesburg again?"

"That's hard to say. I'm stuck here until the police are convinced I'm not a killer."

"Of course. I'm sure that won't take much longer. I picked up a bottle of wine to give you the next time you're here, apple wine, I think it is. Have you had it before?"

"Yes," I responded. "It's delightful. That is very thoughtful. I hope to see you soon."

"Oh, me too. Let me know when you can stop by."

Talking to Ruby always calms me down, like a shot of tequila after a Colombian border crossing.

"Please continue," Jefferson said, standing near the front door, arms crossed and glaring at me.

"Care for some whiskey?" I asked.

"Later. Go on."

"Fine. After Miguel and Cody left, I was wide awake.

I knew I wasn't going to be able to sleep, so I went to the casino to kill some time, hoping booze and more time with annoying people might be enough to finish me for the night. I started with a couple hundred dollars worth of chips and sat at a blackjack table between a man in a Hawaiian shirt and dark sunglasses and a big-boned woman draped in an orange sundress."

"You never play blackjack," Jefferson interrupted. "You hate gambling. You won't even buy a damn lottery ticket."

"I know. That was part of the attraction. I wanted to try something different, and do something that might take a little concentration, so I could get my mind to think about something besides the outline for my story about Miguel and his gangster roots. I did OK at the table for a while, winning about as much as I was losing, but I wasn't getting tired at all, just more and more bored. Somewhere during that time I got a text from Miguel telling me he'd had a lot of fun and couldn't wait to hang out again. I sent a quick response basically saying 'ditto'."

"I guess you made a good impression," Jefferson said.

"You know me—I'm all about the charm. Maybe punching that pain-in-the-ass Cody helped, too. I responded to Miguel's text so quickly that he realized I was still awake and at the casino; he asked if he could join me. He had managed to get Cody home and on the couch and, after a 'you bitch' or two, Cody finally passed out. Miguel, though, was ready to keep going."

"Let me guess: this is another one of those details you didn't feel a need to tell the cops about," Jefferson said.

"Yeah. I left out that bit."

"That's not very smart, Frank. The casinos have cameras everywhere—fucking everywhere. Someone's gonna go check the tapes and see you with Miguel at the casino, and it's not gonna look good for you. You think you look suspicious now, just wait 'til someone sees you on tape at the casino with Miguel."

"Yeah, yeah; I know. I was hoping that, by the time the cops figured out that Miguel met me at the casino, that the real killer would have been caught."

"Everything you hold back is slowing us down. You want to get out of this mess or not?" Jefferson grimaced and turned away. He was losing patience, something he never had in abundance, anyway.

"Of course I do."

He closed his eyes for a moment, took a deep breath—something I taught him—and turned back to me. "Of course, you do, even if you don't act like it. So tell me what happened when Miguel got to the casino."

"Most of the action in the casino takes place in two big rooms, so it didn't take long for Miguel to find me. I noticed that he got a little bit of a hassle from security when he came in. It had cooled down outside, so he'd changed into a purple hoodie, a college sweatshirt emblazoned with the words South Texas College on the front and a big picture of a jaguar on the back. Security wouldn't let him in until he flipped the hoodie off his head."

"Casinos are picky about things like that," Jefferson said.

"As they should be, I guess. He came over to the

blackjack table where I had camped out, and we got to gambling. At first, it was just dollar bets, but we were relaxed and enjoying each other's company and before long we were egging each other on and our bets started going up. My $5 bet became $10, then $20, then $50. I won a few times and watched my stack of chips grow taller. Miguel wasn't doing so well, so I slid him some chips to keep him going. I don't know how to explain it, but I felt something I haven't felt in a while: confidence—cockiness, honestly. I began to feel like there was no way I could lose, at least on that night. So I got bolder. I bumped up my bets to $100. I felt nervous about the amount of money I was betting, but a couple of quick wins reassured me and kept me in the game. By then Miguel was broke again, but he was telling me that this was my lucky night and encouraging me to bet more and more. I felt great. I was having fun. I was getting high from the attention, the winning, the risk, and the booze." I paused, looked at Jefferson, and tried in vain to keep a smile from melting away.

"Then the inevitable happened. My luck ran out and I lost a couple of hands, big bets, then a few more hands after that. I should have known better, but I just couldn't stop. I wanted to feel that high again, to watch my stack of chips grow, to impress Miguel. I told myself to keep riding the confidence bandwagon, and I'd start winning again, so I went to the ATM and got more cash. My stack of chips went up temporarily but quickly shrank lower and lower again until, in one final desperate move, I bet everything I had left. By the time I finally stopped myself, I realized I was almost two thousand dollars in the hole. Two grand. Last month I made two grand—my income for the whole month was two grand!—and here I just lost it in a couple of hours at a blackjack table. I felt shell-shocked and disgusted with myself. We went over to the bar; I needed relief and a chance to get my head back together."

"You had money left after that?"

"That's what credit cards are for, Brian. I ordered a couple of shots of Macallan 12-year-old scotch. If you're gonna go out, go big."

"You should have just left."

"Of course, and a lot sooner. But I didn't. We sat in silence for a couple of minutes, Miguel answering more texts—who the hell was he texting at that time of the morning?—while I wondered how I was going to tell Miguel that I'd been courting him all night because I wanted to write a story about his connection to John Looney. I was starting to freak out. Real panic was setting in. I wasn't sure if I was going to have enough cash for the rest of the week, much less to pay bills next month, and I was worried that I might have just scared off Miguel with that grand display of losing. After Miguel put his phone down, he tried to console me."

****

"Did I tell you why I wanted to be a chiropractor?" Miguel asked me.

"You said you didn't want to go to med school."

Miguel smiled. "Yeah, that was part of it, but there's more to it. A couple of years ago I was in an accident that really messed me up, especially my back. It wasn't too long after I got busted, so I was beginning to think I was on the fast track to hell. My body recovered pretty fast, except for my back. So I went to this chiropractor in McAllen to see if he could do anything. At our first meeting he asked a lot of questions about me and my life, not just health problems I'd had. I didn't tell him everything, at least not the first time. He was really patient with me, explaining exactly what he was about to do so I'd be comfortable, like just before the first time he snapped my neck. That took some getting used to," he chuckled.

"You won't get an argument from me about that," I said. "The first time I had that done, I was sure I was going to end up in a wheelchair."

"Me too. He was real good, though. Whatever he did worked. It took a while, but every week I felt a little better. And every week I told him a little more about my life. I stopped needing the treatments after about three months, so we started hanging out for lunch. I looked up to him, like a father. Honestly, I felt like I finally found a father, or at least someone who acted like one. I got good advice from him, but mostly what I found was someone who believed in me, believed that I was going to be OK. So I decided I should be a chiropractor, too, just like him, so I could help people, just like he did."

I must have looked really damn pathetic if a college student felt the need to cheer me up.

"I know that you don't need advice from someone like me, but I could tell when we first met that you were cool. I have a feeling that everything's going to work out good for you. You just have to hang in there, wait out the bad stuff, like I'm doing."

****

"I thanked him for trying to reassure me," I said to Jefferson. "We sipped a little more scotch. Miguel then said he had an idea, something that might help. I think he felt responsible, at least in part, with the way he kept pushing me to bet more and more." I walked toward the small fridge in my room. If Jefferson was unhappy about what I had told him to this point, I was afraid that he might blow a gasket when I told him the next part of the story. "Care for some whiskey now?"

"Uh-oh. I can tell from how you're acting that this is going to be bad," Jefferson said. "I'd better sit down. And, yes. Give me some of that rye." He walked over to the chair, then changed his mind and sat on the bed.

I poured a couple of shots, handed him a cup, and shot half of the rye. It burned on the way down, forcing a couple of shallow coughs. I was ready to continue. "Miguel floated an idea."

****

"Look, Frank, I think I know a way that we can get that money back. I thought of it earlier and am starting to second-guess myself, but I think it will work."

"What's the idea?"

"I have a stash of pot in my backpack that I was going to sell. I can cut you in for half."

"Isn't it a bad idea for someone in your position to be selling drugs?"

"Probably. I need the money, though. I don't come from a rich family. And it's not like I do it often. I have a few people I supply every week, that's all. Hey, I don't need a lecture from you about it, anyway. Do you want the help or not?"

"Why would you do that, just give me half the money?"

"I feel bad, responsible, I guess. I feel like you lost all that money because I was encouraging you to go on. I should have told you to stop when you had that big stack of chips. Besides, I'm OK right now, money-wise, so I can get by with half of what I normally make. You look like you need money right now."

****

"The money would have been a big help, and it didn't seem very risky," I told Jefferson.

"Only to you, Frank, would selling pot in the middle of the night not seem risky," Jefferson said.

"I wasn't thinking clearly, OK? I admit it. So I asked what I'd have to do. Miguel said that I'd just have to drive him to Suiter Park, and he'd take care of everything."

"What the fuck," Jefferson interrupted. "He wanted you to take him to that park in the middle of the night so he could sell drugs?"

"I suppose since we went from one state to another—Iowa to Illinois—that that was probably a bad thing, too."

"You freak me out sometimes, Frank. This whole night is one giant cluster fuck. I'm surprised that you weren't the one who was killed in the park. So you did it, I guess, you took him to the park?"

I finished the rest of the whiskey in my cup. "Yeah. I did."

Frank jumped up and stormed around the room. "Damn it, Frank. This is a new low for you, and I didn't think that was possible. Goddamn. You took him to the park where he was killed? What the fuck were you thinking?" He paced back and forth a couple of times, took a couple more deep breaths, then told me to go on.

I cleared my throat and continued. "Miguel disappeared for a few minutes to make the arrangements for the sale, so we drove across the river again to Suiter Park. He asked me to wait in the car. He was sure that he'd be back in a few minutes. He said he just needed to hand off the bag and get the cash. Easy. He'd done it a hundred times, he assured me."

"He pulled a plastic bag out of his backpack and left, crossing the old iron truss bridge into the park and disappearing in the darkness. I waited. And waited. After half an hour, he still hadn't come back. I was getting worried, wondering what I should do. I finally got a text from him about, I don't know, half an hour after I dropped him off. He said he'd left something behind; could I grab his backpack and bring it to him? I was getting nervous sitting in the car by myself at that time of the morning, so I said yes. He sent another text with directions to cross the bridge and follow the trail to the left, that if I kept walking around the curve I'd find him. That was the last message I got from him."

"So that was the 5am text?" Jefferson asked.

"That was it. I reached into the back seat to grab the backpack and saw his necklace on the floor mat, the silver necklace his father gave him, so I picked it up and put it in my pocket before I grabbed the backpack. Once I got out of the car, I took my time looking around. The parking lot is in an isolated area on the edge of the city, sandwiched between a power sub-station and the concrete foundation of an old factory. There's hardly any traffic during the day and none after dark. In the light of the day, the area probably isn't too creepy, but at that time, in the early morning, all I could think about was how easily zombies could sneak up on me and how I'd have nowhere to go; I'd be trapped. I've obviously seen too many horror flicks. After a couple of minutes of checking things out, I didn't see any zombies or anyone else, so I crossed the bridge and went into the park."

"You're killing me here, Frank, fucking killing me. Shit, my phone's ringing." Jefferson pulled it from his pocket. "Gotta take this one, it's Starck, the FBI agent."

"Hey. I want to be in on the next conversation with him," I whispered.

He turned and walked away from me, ignoring me as he took the call. Agent Starck was in the area and had a few minutes to swing by. Jefferson agreed to wait for him, so we moved to his room.

20

A few minutes later, Agent Starck was knocking on Jefferson's door. He wasn't surprised to see me there, too.

"What can I do for you gentlemen?" he began.

Jefferson got it rolling. "How long ago did you guys bust Miguel for running drugs?"

Starck didn't flinch. "Nice to see you again, St. Louis. Wasn't sure if our paths would cross again, after you quizzed me at the conference. Look, I can't tell you everything about Ramirez, but, yes, we busted him trying to transport drugs from Mexico to the US. That was probably two years ago."

"What did you catch him with?" Jefferson asked.

"Nearly a hundred kilos of marijuana."

"Nice. That would keep a lot of college kids high for a long time," Jefferson said, turning to me and chuckling. At least he remembered I was still there. "How exactly did you get him? Informant? Surveillance?"

Agent Starck paused before answering. "He came to us by chance, honestly. He was involved with some folks we'd been watching. He wasn't our target at first, but it didn't take us long to figure out that he was someone we should pay more attention to. We watched him closely for a while, then grabbed him when he came across the border with a loaded truck. I can't say any more than that."

"And then you decided to turn him into an informant instead of throwing him in jail?"

"Basically, yes. Before we made the bust, we'd talked about the possibility. We thought a young man in his position and with his promise—he was smart and did well in school—might be willing to provide us with a little information rather than spending the prime years of his life in a prison."

"That makes sense," Jefferson nodded as he turned to look at me. "That's why the Moline police couldn't find any record of Miguel being arrested. You kept all that hush-hush as long as he was helping you out. How much longer were you expecting his assistance?" Jefferson asked.

"We didn't have a specific time table with Ramirez. As long as he could help us, he would."

"When did you find out he was related to John Looney?"

Agent Starck laughed. "The first time I met him. When we arrested him, he went in panic mode, begging for a way out. He wouldn't stop talking." Starck switched to a whiny, high-pitched voice: "I'm not cut out for this. I can't believe I got busted. This should have never happened. I'm not like my grandfather. I shouldn't be trying to live like him." Miguel sounded nothing like that. Starck was mocking Miguel, and it pissed me off.

"He told me his grandfather's name was John Looney, a name I recognized because I worked in organized crime for a while. I agreed with him, told him that he really wasn't cut out for the life of a crook, but a crime was a crime, and he had to pay for what he did. He begged for us to cut him a break, wondering if there was anything he could do to help us out, offering to share information about his crime buddies if we would make the charges go away. So we took him in, threw him in jail for a night to make sure he was really ready to cooperate, then made an offer."

Jefferson nodded, staring intently at Starck. "I guess that all makes sense. Sounds like you had it all well-planned."

"Thanks. We don't act impulsively, you know. Enough questions for me. I don't have a lot of time. How are you, Mr. Dodge?" Starck pivoted in my direction.

"Been better," I said.

"I was curious about something, Mr. Dodge. I noticed that you and Miguel were friends on Facebook. It looks like he accepted your friend request a few days before you said you met him. Actually, he accepted a friend request from someone named Steve Smith from Geneseo, who claimed to be a second year student at Dickey. It took a little digging, but I found out that Steve Smith was actually you."

"You used a fake profile?" Jefferson asked.

"Yeah, I used a fake profile to learn about him. I wouldn't have done it without your tip that Miguel was related to John Looney, though," I said as I turned to Agent Starck. "I needed to figure out how to find him if I was going to write about him, so I looked him up on Facebook. I couldn't learn much about him unless I was in his network, though, so I sent a friend request using the fake profile. I figured he would be more likely to accept a friend request from another Dickey student than from an older guy he never met who lived in a different city. I don't think it's a big deal."

"You might be right, Dodge, but using a fake profile to track a guy on Facebook could look suspicious, especially after he turns up dead. Like I told you earlier, Dodge, I'm inclined to think you are innocent here, but some might say that your actions on Facebook suggest premeditation."

Was Starck trying to help me out, or set a trap? "Miguel would never have known. And if I'd known that someone was going to kill him, I would have rethought that friend request."

"Of course. It makes sense to me. I just hope it makes sense to the Moline police, too, when they find out. That fake Facebook profile and those muddy boots don't help your case, Dodge. They make it look like you're hiding something; when you're a murder suspect—an innocent one, anyway—transparency is a good practice. I hope there's nothing else you're trying to hide." He winked at me, then walked toward the door. "Gentlemen, it's been a pleasure to chat, but I need to move on."

What else did he know about that night? Had he found out that Miguel met me at the casino? I felt panic creeping in; without thinking, I barked out: "Agent Starck, when did you move away from the Quad Cities? You grew up in Moline, right?"

The agent stopped at the door, reaching for the door knob as he turned around. "Yes. I grew up in Moline, but the FBI had plans for me that didn't include the Quad Cities. I've been away for a while." He was staring intently at me, sizing me up.

"It must have been tough growing up in a family with a tarnished reputation. A cop that committed murder—man, that has to foul the whole clan."

Starck turned red but held himself in check. He let go of the door knob and walked back toward me. "You didn't do a very good job with your research, Dodge. My father didn't murder anyone. He was never charged with anything. He killed a man who was threatening him, who was a threat to the community, and the justice system recognized those facts. My father was not a criminal; he did what he had to do." He walked back to the door. "You know, Dodge. I'm inclined to believe you are innocent, but I'm beginning to doubt my instincts now. I don't know why an innocent man would try to provoke someone who's trying to help him. Stunts like that will only make people like me take a closer look at you, and everything you and Miguel did the night he was killed. I'd be careful, if I was you." With that, he turned around and left.

"What the hell was that?" Jefferson yelled.

"A hunch. Ruby called a little while ago and mentioned that she thought there was a Moline cop named Starck who got in trouble a few years ago, shot and killed someone who was accused of molesting kids. I haven't had time to check on it, but with Starck right here, I thought I'd make a play. I guess they're kin."

"You think so?" Jefferson walked over to me. "Look, Frank, I don't know what you thought you were doing, what you thought that little tidbit of family history might mean, but we don't want to make an enemy of Starck. He's right about being careful. He can do you a lot of harm, Frank. Understand?"

"I get the message. I was just getting a little worried about what he was saying. I wanted to go on the offensive for a change, change the subject, especially with an opportunity in front of me."

"Anyway, I think you've still got some important details for me, like telling me exactly what happened when you got to the park."

I sighed and said, "Sit down."

21

I had been dreading this moment. I knew I'd have to tell Jefferson at some point, but I didn't mind that it had taken a while to get there. I reached in the small fridge and pulled out a couple of beers. It wasn't noon yet, but I already felt like I'd had a full day. Jefferson sat on the bed; I handed him a beer and sat in the desk chair, turning it in his direction.

"Ah, shit, Frank. What the hell did you do?"

"By the time I got to the park," I began, "the rain was just beginning to fall, lightly at first. I was wearing a windbreaker for cover and carried the backpack over my shoulder as I tried to find my way around in the dark. There's a single-span steel truss bridge that crosses a canal, a tailrace built in the late 1800s for a power plant. I hurried across the bridge, trying to quickly get through the smell of rotting fish that was oozing up from the canal. The gate on the island side was open, although it looked like it wasn't supposed to be."

"Did it look like it had been broken open?" Jefferson asked.

"No, not really. I didn't see a lock. It was as if someone had shut the gate but forgot to padlock it. There was nothing to stop me, or anyone, from lifting the latch and walking on through."

"What did you see after you got on the island?"

"When I got across the bridge, I entered a small open field that had a couple of statues sculpted from material salvaged from the massive steel factory that once sprawled across the island. In the dark, they looked like multi-tentacled monsters, but I'd been there before and knew what they looked in daylight; that part didn't bother me. The park is crisscrossed by low concrete walls, remnants of the plant's foundation that scar the landscape; the walls lean in one direction or another, pushed by tree roots and a thicket of bushes that are slowly reclaiming land that was once theirs. Several trails branch off from the bridge, but I followed Miguel's directions and took the path to the left. I didn't expect to see him right away, but, after walking west for a few minutes I hadn't caught even a hint that he was nearby. I walked slowly, getting spooked a few times by the sound of a bird taking flight or the wind blowing through the bare tree limbs, but otherwise I didn't hear a thing. It's amazing how easily the quiet can settle in the middle of a big city. I scanned the scene in front of me carefully, looking down to make sure that I avoided stepping on branches or trail debris that might get me noticed prematurely, all while trying to look out for any sign of Miguel. I froze when I saw a figure a few feet ahead of me that seemed to be moving back and forth, like someone was waving at me. It stopped moving when the wind died down, and, as I got closer, I realized it was just the trunk of a young maple tree. That's when I heard your voice in my head," I said, looking at Jefferson, "calling me stupid and telling me to get the hell out of there."

"Frank, you fuckin' amaze me. So you're wandering

around an isolated park in the dark of the early morning while carrying a backpack that was probably full of drugs that you were going to give to a guy you barely knew, who wanted to sell them and give you some of the cash to settle a gambling loss, right? Just what part of that did you think was a dumb idea?"

"Well, sometimes you get so deep in the forest, you forget how you got there. So I kept going—I was worried about Miguel—but, believe me, my head was rotating all over the place, trying to watch my step and look out for anyone who might sneak up on me. When I got near the western edge of the island, just about where a path turns to the right, the view opened up, and that's when I thought I saw him."

"Thought?"

"Yeah. I could have sworn that I saw someone up ahead. As I crept closer, the figure seemed to melt into a large oak tree, but I was so sure at first that I saw a person. I figured I was just jumpy, seeing things that weren't really there. The rain was getting heavier and louder and the water was beginning to run down my neck and back; I could feel my clothes getting damp and my patience thinning. Then I looked to my left and saw something in the water, maybe fifty feet from the shore. I don't know; I'm not very good at estimating distance. Even in the dark, there was something familiar about that shape in the water."

"Go on," Jefferson said, although I could barely hear him.

"I stopped and tried to focus in on the object, wiping off my glasses a couple of times to see more clearly. I thought it was a piece of driftwood at first, at least until I got a better look at it. As I inched forward, I realized it was a body floating face down in the slough. My pulse picked up. I was torn between running away and getting closer, but my curiosity won out. As I crept to the edge of the water, I could make out a heavy piece of clothing. It looked like a sweatshirt, and as I focused more on it I recognized a pattern on the back—a jaguar. That body in the water was Miguel—it had to be."

"Damn it, Frank. You should have told me about that right away," Jefferson exploded, jumping up from the bed.

"I wanted to, really, I did, but I was hoping they'd catch the real killer before I had to."

"You keep saying that! If you'd told me this right away, maybe we'd have the killer by now." Jefferson rubbed his temples; I gave him a headache. "Go on."

"I didn't know what to do. I paced along the bank. I couldn't believe it was happening again, that someone might have died in the river because of me. My thoughts raced. He was too far away for me to reach him without going all the way in the water. I looked around and didn't see anyone, so I whispered his name, cupping my hands around my mouth, hoping that this pathetic gesture would direct my voice at him and only him, that whoever threw him in the water wouldn't hear me. I didn't get an answer, though. I found a couple of pebbles and tossed them at his body, hitting him on the back with one of them. No reaction. I looked around, trying to figure out if anyone might have seen me, then I freaked out some more. We came here to sell drugs to a buyer I knew nothing about and now Miguel's lying in the water, unconscious and, in all likelihood, dead. What the hell would you have done?" I looked to Jefferson.

"I wouldn't have been there in the first place, remember?" Jefferson said, firmly. Then his voice softened, and he told me: "But if I was, I'd probably feel panicked, but just a little. What did you do next?"

"I got the hell out of there. I figured I'd be in more trouble if I went in the water and pulled him out or if I called the cops. How was I going to explain any part of that night: tracking him down for a story about his gangster grandfather, feeding him drinks all night, losing a bunch of cash in a casino, and pulling his body out of Suiter Slough at that time of the morning? 'Sorry officer, we were trying to sell some drugs to pay for the gambling losses. Guess it got out of hand.'

"I also had enough sense to realize that whoever did that to him could still be around and might come after me. I turned around and left before I was discovered. Brian, I don't really know that he was dead at that point. What if he wasn't? Maybe I could have saved his life. I should have at least tried. I was totally selfish and stupid and now Miguel's dead." I cried, for the first time in years, I cried. I covered my face with my hands. "I don't deserve to be here. I should have tried to save him, I ran away instead, like a coward. I'm a fucking coward."

"Shit, Frank. You're not a coward, but you're not exactly a hero, either. Damn, this changes everything. I'm not sure I know you, anymore. I don't know what was going through that over-educated mind of yours. I need to think about where to go with this. It's a mess. It's a big

160

fuckin' mess." Jefferson took a deep breath, then walked over to me and put an arm around my shoulder, escorting me, pushing me, really, to the door. "Go back to your room, Frank. Get some rest. Stay out of trouble. I'll get in touch with you in a couple of hours."

I went back to my room, worried I'd lost Jefferson, wondering if I could have saved Miguel, remembering the other person I lost to the river.

22

When I was a kid, I spent every day on the river, usually with a friend or two. In summer, we'd spend hours paddling around the backwaters, exploring them like we were the first people to see it. Sometimes we'd stop to fish or swim, but mostly we floated around and tried to find something that we hadn't seen before, like a giant snapping turtle or a paddlefish.

Every now and then, though, my little sister, Tina, would come with me instead. Tina was two years younger than me and something of a tomboy. She was always begging me to let her go along when I went on the river, but I usually found a way to ditch her. She was a good swimmer and all, and knew how to pull herself out of quickmud, and, unlike other girls, she wasn't squeamish about bugs or baiting a hook. She wasn't afraid of getting dirty; in fact, she liked it. I respected her for those things but she was younger and smaller than me, and I didn't want to be slowed down by watching out for her. And she was my sister. I'd have rather gone out by myself than hang out with little sister.

On a Sunday afternoon in late May, just before school was out for the summer, I gave in and let Tina tag along when my buddies were stuck at a family picnic. It was the first really warm day of the season, must have been up around 80 degrees, I think, when we put in the

17-foot canoe and paddled north toward the Black River delta. We had to cross Lake Onalaska to get there, but we paddled close to shore, like we were always told to do; on the open water it doesn't take much wind to whip up waves big enough to swamp a canoe like ours and you don't always see it coming. It was warm and sunny when we started, but as we got to the delta we noticed that the wind was picking up and starting to blow from the north. I could tell that it was going to cool down, but I figured we had a few more hours to play around. I'd been caught in storms on the river before, more times than most folks have even seen the river, so I didn't worry much about it. If the weather turned on us, I'd know how to deal with it.

The delta was dense with life. Silver maples, cottonwoods, and the occasional swamp white oak dominated the upper reaches, while wood nettles, poison ivy, and mosquitoes spread out underneath. Beavers and otters staked out their territories; snakes feasted on frogs and mice. It's easy to get lost in those woods. You can't see very far ahead in any direction and, until you learn to look closely, all the trees and bushes seem identical. You can feel like you're confined in a small maze, even though you're in the middle of thousands of acres of wild country.

When we got to the delta, we grounded the canoe and took a quick swim; the water was still too cold to stay in for a long time. We spotted otter tracks in the mud and followed them until they disappeared in a marsh, where we found three turtles atop a dead tree trunk craning to grab a few rays of warmth from the sunlight that was breaking through the trees. The ground was still soggy from the spring rise, but it was falling back faster than usual.

It wasn't until a few big branches cracked and fell near us that we realized the wind was picking up. We found a clearing and looked up, spotting a bank of coal black clouds moving in our direction. We had wandered so deep into the shelter of the delta that the wind had felt like a pleasant spring breeze to us. In the clearing, we realized that the wind had picked up and was blowing hard enough to give us trouble on our way back home.

If I'd been with friends, we would have built a makeshift shelter and waited for the worst of the storm to pass, but I wasn't crazy about riding it out with Tina; I figured it would be work, not fun. I'd have to look out for her, and I didn't know what I'd do with her, what we could talk about, if we were stuck for a couple of hours in close quarters.

So we decided to make a break for it. We ran back to the canoe, getting wet as the rain began to break through the canopy. We pushed off and out of the delta. We hadn't lost the shelter of the trees but a couple of minutes when the wind grabbed the front of the canoe, whipping it around nearly 90 degrees. Tina reacted quickly—she had good reflexes—grabbing the gunwales to save herself from getting dumped into the river. In the process of steadying herself, though, she let go of her paddle and it splashed into the river.

I yelled at her, telling her to reach out and grab the paddle—we wouldn't get far with just one paddle in the middle of a storm. She turned to look at me, her face as white as November snow, but I didn't have time to coddle

her. I yelled at her again—"Grab the damn paddle!"—
and swung the canoe around so she could reach out for
it. She moved slowly, stretching her arms tentatively
while trying to maintain her balance. The paddle was
just beyond her hand. I leaned to her side of the canoe
so she could reach a little further, but she wasn't ready for
that. She lost her balance and fell in. The canoe popped
up as she went out, and the wind grabbed it and tossed it
around. I nearly went in myself, but I found my balance
and looked around, trying to figure out where she had
surfaced. I saw her briefly about ten feet away and tried
to maneuver in that direction, but without her weight
in the front, I couldn't control the canoe. The wind was
blowing me away from where she went in and back toward shore, and there wasn't a thing I could do to fight it.

When I hit the bank, I jumped out of the canoe and
ran along the shore, yelling "Tina" and looking for her
in the water, but the wind was blowing the rain sideways
and stinging my eyes, so I couldn't see but a few feet in
front of me. I wanted to jump in and swim out to her, but
I didn't know which way I'd go once I got in the water. I
watched and waited as the rain carved micro-channels in
the mud around me, hoping to catch sight of her, but as
the north wind swept in colder air, I felt more desperate.
I had to leave and get help, even though I knew it meant
abandoning her.

I convinced myself that she had found her way
ashore and was probably hunkered down somewhere. I
knew she could hold out for a while if she found some
shelter, but I wasn't going to find her from the riverbank
where I landed. So I turned around and ran back toward

the farms of the floodplain, eventually finding a house where I pled for help.

By the time the sheriff got a couple of boats on the river, the rain was letting up. It didn't help much, though; even their motor boats were a poor match for the wind and high waves; at nightfall, they had to call off the search for their own safety. The sheriff wanted me to stay away, but I spent every minute of daylight out with the search teams, anyway. I left my sister alone out there and wasn't going to slow down until I knew where she was. It took two more days before we found her. I spotted her body, bruised and bloated, lodged in the roots of a silver maple not far from where we had left the delta. I looked into her eyes, still open but vacant, and cried for her and for me, then I cried for the river; I knew that I'd never see the Mississippi in the same way again.

My parents blamed me for Tina's death. They never said as much, but, even if they had, I wouldn't have argued the point. They sold the canoe and the bait shop, and we moved to St. Louis where they kept me on a short leash: curfew at dusk, no overnights with friends, and no more river time.

Dad worked at Scullin Steel and did well enough that he made a few contacts that came in handy when the plant closed a couple of years later. He was a reliable electrician but, after Tina's death, he was nothing more than a recliner with a 12-pack to me. Every evening when he got home, he'd head directly to his chair in the den and drink beer—Budweiser, he couldn't even pick a good beer—until he fell asleep. Mom sat on the couch reading or crocheting, ignoring him and speaking to my little brother and me only when she needed something done. "Mark, get those dishes washed, now!" "Frank, put down that book and cut the grass." After Mark finished high school, my parents split up; dad moved back to Wisconsin but mom stayed in St. Louis. And none of that would have happened if I hadn't caused my sister's death.

23

I might have spent hours replaying the day of my sister's death in my mind, but a knock on the door brought me out of my head. Maybe Jefferson had come back to my room to talk about our strategy from this point on, or, more likely, to get on my case some more. He walked in without looking at me. I assumed he was too disappointed to look at me directly. "Nice to see you, too," I said.

"Look, Frank, I don't want to rehash what you did on Friday night. That's not why I'm here. I'm not ready to get into that again, but I wanted to tell you that I've been holding out on you, too, although nowhere near like what you were holding back from me," he said. "I've been doing a little extracurricular work of my own."

"I shouldn't be surprised. What exactly have you been up to, Brian?"

"I went to the Crooked Spine last night, on my own, hoping to meet that bartender you mentioned."

"Noah? How'd that go?"

"He was there. Quite a character, too. It wasn't busy, just a couple of people at the bar, so I grabbed a stool and made myself comfortable. He came over right away."

We each found a place to sit and Jefferson told me about his night at the Crooked Spine.

****

168

I found an empty stool around the middle of the bar. It didn't take long to get noticed.

"What can I get ya?" the bartender asked me.

"Beam, on the rocks."

"On the way." He set a glass in front of me, a generous pour, and introduced himself.

"Name's Noah. Don't think we've met."

"Brian. Nah, it's my first time here, first time in Davenport, too."

"What brings you here?"

"Came to visit a friend for a couple of days, to get away from home."

"I suppose there are worse places to be. Where's home?"

"Chicago, now anyway. Moved around a few times." I didn't want to tell him the truth; I thought he might be suspicious if another guy from St. Louis showed up at his bar.

"I've been over there a few times. Fun place to visit; not sure I could live there, though. Davenport is big enough for my tastes."

"Believe me, there are times I hate it, too. For one thing, it's not very often you walk into a neighborhood bar in Chicago and find just a couple of barstools occupied. Is it always so quiet here?"

"Depends. Sundays are usually slow, though sometimes it picks up later, like around 11. We get a lot of students from the chiropractic school down the street, so we get busy when they aren't."

I was hungry, so I got a menu from Noah. They've got some crazy food there. I went with the Lumbar Burger—

damn that was a good burger—and we got back to talking after I washed up.

"What kind of work do you do, Brian?" Noah asked.

"Insurance. Nothing all that interesting. How about you? You got anything else going on besides bartending?"

"Not work-wise. I play music with a couple of friends, mostly just us fooling around. Maybe we'll get serious some day. What kind of music are you into?"

"I'm a Soul Train kind of guy. Grew up with it and don't feel the need to get away from it. Mix it with a good woman and a little bud and you've got the perfect night."

"Not gonna get an argument from me," Noah said. He turned around to grab the Beam bottle, refilled my glass, and poured a little for himself.

"Your wife have the same tastes?"

"Similar, at least when we met. I'm not so sure what music she listens to now. Fact is, things aren't so good between us. She's pushing for a separation."

"Sorry about that. You got kids?"

"Two; both girls, both teenagers."

"Sounds like you've got your hands full."

"That's why I'm here. I needed a break. I don't suppose there's anywhere around here that I might find music tonight, huh?"

"We don't usually have much music on Sunday nights, live music, anyway. There might be a show down the street at the Antoine House, but this ain't Chicago, you know."

"That's OK. I didn't expect to find it. So tell me about this place. You worked here a while?"

"A couple of years. It's an easy place to work. Every now and then I gotta run someone out for getting too rowdy, but not too often."

"Those college kids can get out of hand, I bet."

"Not just them. Some of my happy hour guys can get out of hand, too. I've had to toss guys old enough to be my grandpa. The students don't usually give me trouble, though, except for a couple of Mexicans. I keep a close eye on them."

"Sometimes it seems like this country's getting overrun by Mexicans," I said, giving my Beam a little swirl.

"Some of 'em are alright, I suppose, but not the ones that come in here. One of them turned up dead a couple of days ago, in fact, so I'd say I was right in keeping an eye on him." Noah pivoted to the sink and washed a couple of glasses.

"Dead, huh. What happened?"

"Someone killed him and dumped his body in the river." Noah said, without looking up.

"I thought that shit only happened in Chicago."

"Yeah, well sometimes people get what they have coming, even in the Quad Cities. He was in here a lot, supposedly at the chiropractic college, but I didn't really believe him. Seemed like he was here to sell pot to my customers. I admit, I bought a bag or two from him when I was in a pinch, but I never trusted him. When he jacked up his price a couple of weeks ago, I knew my instincts were right on. Claimed it was really good weed, so it was worth more, but it seemed like the same stuff I got from my regular guy."

"That sounds shady. Still, doesn't really sound like a

reason to kill a guy, does it?"

"Maybe not, but if he was willing to fuck with me, imagine how many other people he might have been fucking with, too. Maybe one of them wasn't as level-headed as me." He looked up at me and noticed my empty glass. "You want another?"

"Nah. I should stop. Still have to drive back to my friend's place. I wouldn't mind picking up some weed, though, for the rest of my vacation. Suppose you could hook me up with your guy?"

"I could check with him, see what he thinks. How much longer are you gonna be here?"

"At least a couple more days."

"Stop by tomorrow. I'm here from 6 to close. I'll let you know then."

****

"I don't see how Miguel could be a regular dealer, Brian," I said, "with his history with the FBI and all. It doesn't make sense to me."

"I don't know, Frank. From what you've told me, Miguel might have the same need to take stupid risks as you do. I thought the bartender's story seemed plausible. I don't know why he'd lie to me about it. Still, I don't take people at face value. You know that. So I went back when the bar closed, so I could tail him. I was surprised at where he went."

24

We walked across the street to Donna's Diner for a quick lunch. Ashley served us coffee and a couple of "huns" to get us started. "You call me the risk-taker, Brian, but spying on a bartender who you just spent an evening chatting with sounds like a big risk to me."

"Not really, that kind of risk is just part of what I do; I'm trained for it. The risks you take, well, that's part of who you are; you're impulsive. Big difference."

"Maybe, or then again maybe you just tell yourself that's the case, to reassure yourself. I think there's a lot more risk-taker in you than you like to admit."

Jefferson looked at me and grinned. "So do you want to hear what happened when I followed Noah or not?"

"Of course. Go on; tell me about how you used that training of yours to stay out of trouble."

"I will. Pay attention, Frank. I parked on the street just down from the bar, waiting for Noah to leave. It was really quiet around there. No traffic, stoplights flashing red, felt like a ghost town."

"That's why I went to the casino. There's not much else to do when the bars close."

"Yeah, I figured that out. It made it easy to watch Noah leave, but not so easy to follow him. I had to stay back further than I wanted, trying to keep pace without getting his attention. Lucky for me, he didn't go very far.

About a mile from the bar, he parked in front of a brick apartment building, pushed a call button and got buzzed in. He wasn't up there more than 15 minutes when he came back out and drove away. I knew right away where he was, though. I remembered the address from the police reports. It was where Miguel lived."

"You mean the apartment he shared with Cody?" I sat down on the bed.

"Yes."

"Maybe Noah went there to see someone else; the address might be a coincidence."

"Possible, but not likely. I don't believe in coincidence. He went there to see Cody, and that probably means Cody was his 'regular guy' to get weed from. If I'm right, I'll have some weed waiting for me this evening when I go back to the Crooked Spine."

"You're going back there?"

"Why not? Noah expects me to be there and doesn't have a clue who I am. It'll give me a chance to find out a little more about these two."

"Where did Noah go after he left Cody's place?"

"Hah. It gets even better. He drove across the river. Crossing the bridge, I was worried that he might notice me, but I don't think he did; there were a couple of other cars on the bridge with us, so I wasn't too obvious. When we got into Rock Island, he turned left. It felt like we drove for a long time, especially since I was worried about losing him every time he turned, which was a lot."

"He was probably just following the main route through town. That road changes direction a lot."

"Whatever. It made it tricky to follow him without

getting noticed, but at least we picked up a few more cars on that side of the river, made it easier for me to blend in. I thought he was going to drive forever, but after another left turn and crossing some railroad tracks, I saw him turn into a small parking lot just a block off the road. After I passed by the lot, I parked on the side of the road and walked around the corner. I saw him walking toward a small iron bridge, with a small pack hanging from a shoulder."

"That sounds like Suiter Park," I jumped in.

"Yeah. It was. He crossed the bridge and walked into the park, never slowed down, never looked back. He sure seemed to know where he wanted to go. I waited for about 15 minutes, but he hadn't come back by then, so I decided to call it a night." Jefferson's phone made a couple of beeping noises.

"Now what?" He looked down and frowned. "It's a text from Michelle. I'd better call her. She's not happy that I'm here. She thinks I should have stayed home and used my time off to work out our issues." Jefferson shook his head, just slightly. "I don't know, Frank. I think we may be too far gone. I can't get her to see that I can't help what I gotta do. Your ass is on the line here. You need my help and you need it now. If I didn't come up here, you'd probably end up in prison for murder. Michelle and I, we can talk more when I get home. There'll be time, if she'd just be patient. If she'd just be patient."

"Sorry, Frank. I didn't know that things had gotten rough between you two. What can I do? Would it help if I talked to Michelle?"

"That's the worst idea you've had in a long time,

Frank. She's just as pissed at you right now as she is at me." He laughed. "Enough about all that. It's a distraction. We've still got a lot of work to do to figure out what's going on." He stood up and took one more sip of coffee. "I need to brief my buddy with the Moline PD about what I found out. Compare notes, and all that, so I'm going to head out. Can you take care of the check? I'll get the next one."

"Sure. I got this."

"Thanks. I'll call you later. Keep your head low."

I wasn't at all that surprised that Jefferson's marriage was in trouble. After he met Michelle at Pete's Diner he spent a long time chasing after her, while she spent a long time running him in circles. Michelle was his ideal match, thin with dark chocolate skin, elegant but tough; it took him a while to convince Michelle of the same, if he ever really did. They waited a while to have kids, until Jefferson felt like he was settled into the police department and Michelle was finished with nursing school.

Even after the girls were born, both worked long hours; they were lucky to have Jefferson's mom and Michelle's parents around to help out while they were working. Even when they weren't home, though, they stayed closely involved with their girls. One or both of them talked to the grandparents every day, to get updates and to give directions.

Between the kids and work, they didn't get out much. Every now and then I could convince Jefferson to meet for a happy hour, but I was about the only one. He rarely had drinks with co-workers, and only then if it was a special occasion, like the boss's birthday. As Jefferson got promoted, work took up more and more time, and even I couldn't convince him to hang out; it would mean less time with his family, after all.

I don't know exactly when things changed for them, or even if there was a moment that defined what was happening. All this talk of separation was coming from Michelle, but I don't think she woke up one morning and realized she was unhappy. I imagine that she was just gradually worn down by all the responsibilities and with Jefferson working long hours. Maybe she just felt more and more like she was on her own, anyway, so why not make it official? I don't really know any of this; Michelle and I don't have the kind of relationship to chat about such things, and Jefferson isn't big on talking about his home life or feelings. Even I, long-time friend and trained therapist, have a hard time drawing him out. He has always been more comfortable talking about what he did than how he felt.

After Jefferson left, I was sorting through my notes from the last couple of days, when the phone rang. It was Ruby.

"Frank, I found out more about that police officer from Moline. I was right; it was ten years ago. Leo Starck, a detective with the Moline Police Department, shot and killed a man who was accused of molesting a child, a man named Steve Wriedt. Starck went to Wriedt's home, alone, to arrest him but ended up shooting him instead. Starck claimed self-defense, that Wriedt was coming after him with a large knife, but I don't think the other police officers believed him. I found another story that was in the paper a few weeks later that said he wasn't charged with anything, but that he didn't get to keep his job, either; the article said he was forced to resign."

"You have a good memory, Ruby. Huh. Starck's dad was driven off the police force. That might come in handy."

"Oh, I'm glad. There's more, too. The article about Starck's resignation mentioned that his father, Jerry Starck, had also been a police officer. He had trouble, too, and retired early. The article didn't go into much detail, but it sounds like some prisoners died during Jerry Starck's watch, and, eventually, someone figured out that they weren't accidental. I guess they figured he had something to do with those deaths."

"What a family tradition. Father and son both forced to resign after killing someone." For a change, I was looking forward to talking to Agent Starck. I couldn't wait to ask him more about his family history.

"Thanks, Ruby. I've said it before, and I'll keep saying it: you're amazing."

"Oh, I'm just trying to help. You let me know if you find out anything else."

"Will do."

"Oh I sure hope you can clear this up soon. It's been so long since you've able to stop by for lunch. I miss our conversations. The people in this town just aren't very interesting. Sometimes I get so bored here."

"We need to find you a new hobby, like going through some of those boxes in your living room and throwing things away!"

"Oh you're funny. You know, I opened a couple of boxes just the other day. I think it made things worse.

Now I have magazines and pictures scattered all over the floor."

"Next time I come up there, I'll help you sort through your collection. Maybe I can help you find a few things to get rid of. Talk to you soon, Ruby."

Ruby's research gave me an idea, a person I needed to call who ought to know more about the Starck family.

25

"Hi, I'm trying to reach Steve DeSmet, a reporter. Can you connect me to his extension, please?" I wasn't sure if this was a good idea. After all, I was pretty sure he still saw me as a suspect, and there were a lot of details about Friday night that I hadn't told anyone but Jefferson; I sure wasn't going to give any of that away to a reporter. On the other hand, if anyone was going to know about the Starck family history, it was going to be a cop or reporter from Moline, and I didn't think the cops would be thrilled to talk about a scandal committed by one of their own, especially to a murder suspect in an open case.

"This is Steve DeSmet."

"Hey, it's Frank Dodge, your favorite travel writer." I sat down at the desk in my room.

"What a surprise. I didn't expect to hear from you, Dodge."

"I'm just as surprised to be calling you, but I learned something that I think might interest you. Are you familiar with a family named Starck? I think they've produced a couple of cops that got into some trouble in Moline."

"That's an understatement. Leo Starck killed a child abuse suspect a few years ago, 2002, I think it was. Why are you interested in the Starck family?"

"I'll get to that in just a minute. What happened with Leo Starck?"

"I'll hold you to that. I don't have a lot details, but I was told, off the record, that the investigators concluded that the shooting wasn't justified. The department was afraid of a backlash if they didn't take action, so they forced him to resign, but they let him keep his pension. That part didn't really matter, as it turned out; a stroke killed him a couple of years ago. I think he was only 63 when he died."

"How tragic. What was his motive for the shooting? Why did he shoot the guy?"

"I don't think anyone ever really asked that question. Maybe they didn't want to know. Maybe the cops were just happy to have a child molester off the streets."

"What do you know about the guy he killed?"

"I think it was a guy named Steve Wriedt, a low-level criminal who had been in and out of prison. He hadn't been out for long when he was accused of molesting a neighborhood girl. That's about all I remember of that case."

"Did I hear that Leo Starck's father also got in some trouble?"

"And when do I get to start asking questions?"

"Soon. Just tell me about the father, and you can ask away."

"Trouble seems to follow that family, the Starcks. Leo's father was Jerry Starck. A war hero, served in World War II, an MP, if I remember right. After the war he came back home and got a job in the Moline Police Department working at the jail. At one point, the jail had a spike in inmate deaths, something like four in 18 months. Someone finally figured out that there was a problem, and, long story short, they figured out that the only thing in common was that Jerry Starck was working at the time of each death. I don't think anyone actually accused him of murder, but, even if they did, those were different times. Cops looked out for their own. If there was a bad cop, they'd find a way to show him the door, but very quietly; no publicity."

"That's a lot of corpses. What do you know about the prisoners who died?"

"Nothing, really. I'd have to look that up. There is something more to the story, though."

"Don't let me stop you."

"Jerry Starck's father was murdered when he was a little kid. His mother remarried, a guy named Oscar Starck, who adopted Jerry."

"So who was Jerry Starck's father, the one who was murdered?"

"It was a man named Bill Gabel."

DeSmet's answer surprised me. Bill Gabel was murdered by John Looney. No wonder my friend at the FBI, Agent Starck, knew a lot about Rock Island's gangster; his family had a personal connection.

"So does that help you?"

"Yeah; it helps a lot."

"I'm glad. Don't forget to complete the customer satisfaction survey at the end of this call. Now it's your turn. Tell me something that I don't know, something about the Ramirez case."

"OK. Did you know that Ramirez was busted for transporting drugs across the US border?"

"I heard a rumor about that, yes."

"Well, it's true. After the FBI arrested him, they convinced Miguel to act as an informant, offering him a get-out-of-jail-free card in exchange for wiping his record clean. And here's a bonus tip: Did you know that one of the Starcks works for the FBI?"

"That would be William, Leo's son. Yeah, I know about that. He moved away a long time ago. Got a pretty good position in the FBI, I think."

"Right. Well, William Starck was the FBI agent who handled the Ramirez case in Texas, and Starck is in town right now investigating the kid's death."

"Why would I care about William Starck? If he was the one handling the Ramirez case before, why wouldn't he be here now? Come on, Frank, tell me something useful."

I was hoping that would be enough for DeSmet, that he might get interested in the Starck story and go after it for the local angle, but he obviously needed more. "Fine, but you didn't hear this from me. There's a bartender at the Crooked Spine, Noah, who had dealings with both Miguel and his roommate, Cody. I've talked to him a couple of times. Both of those guys were regulars at the bar. Noah had a grudge against Miguel; I'm not sure why. Noah didn't seem the least bit surprised that Miguel died, in fact, I'd say he had an air of satisfaction about it."

"That's more like it. What did you mean when you said the bartender, Noah, had dealings with Cody and Miguel?"

"That's all I can say about it. I have a bit of advice, though. Tread carefully. I know of at least one other person who's been hanging around the bar and asking questions. If you start doing the same thing, the bartender will probably get spooked."

With that, I hung up and called Jefferson. "I've got some news you're going to like. Our Agent Starck is related to an old nemesis of John Looney: Bill Gabel."

"No shit," Jefferson said. "Starck never mentioned that bit. No wonder he knew so much about Looney. Looks like I'm calling in sick tomorrow."

26

Bill Gabel and John Looney were allies who became enemies. Their relationship got a whole chapter in *Too Looney for the Law*.

> The problem with being at the top of the food chain is that there's always a flounder with a big appetite who wonders what the tuna tastes like, someone else ready to take you down for the same reasons that got you to the top—the hunger for power and money. You have to constantly watch your back, and you can't trust anyone. Looney felt immune to most of those concerns, which is probably a perk—or delusion—inspired by owning the mayor and the police chief. Looney may have felt immune, but he wasn't inoculated against the ambitions and jealousies of his enemies.
>
> William Gabel, a former Rock Island cop turned bar owner, got his Prohibition-era liquor and invisibility through Looney. He ran a soft drink bar on Fourth Avenue where the sodas came with a chaser of gin or whiskey. In the summer of 1922, he objected to the high prices being charged by Looney—$8 a gallon, or about twice what he figured he would have to pay anyone else. Louis Ortell, one of Looney's enforcers, reminded Gabel

that he was buying a package deal, booze plus protection from police and competitors, the gold star package that came with membership in Looney's network. Gabel refused to pay, at least for a while, but he and Looney eventually worked out a new deal. When Gabel resumed his business with Looney, he paid for the bootleg liquor and thugs with a personal check.

It seems especially reckless that Looney would accept payment for moonshine and muscle with a personal check. Maybe he believed he was untouchable, so he didn't give it a second thought. He should have. On July 31, a Monday night, Gabel met a federal agent named R.C. Goss at the Como Hotel in downtown Rock Island and made a deal to turn over twelve cancelled checks endorsed by John Looney.

From Looney's perspective, the new deal with Gabel may have been just a way to buy some time. Looney had been unhappy with Gabel for a while, so when Gabel balked at paying the going rate for his booze, Looney had one more reason to replace him. When Looney got word that Gabel was talking to the feds, though, replacement was no longer his first option. On the Monday night that Bill Gabel was returning to his bar after turning over the checks to the feds, he was ambushed by several men who leapt out of a car. They opened fire, shredding Gabel with a flurry of .38 caliber, brass-jacketed bullets. Gabel fell to the sidewalk and bled to death in minutes. According to later court testimony, the killers included John Looney and his son, Connor. Police Chief Tom Cox was also implicated in the murder.

Cox, police chief from 1919-1922, was perhaps Looney's most valuable ally. Although married, he had a long-term affair with Helen Van Dale, the woman who managed most of Looney's brothels, a cozy arrangement for everyone. The three of them—Looney, Van Dale, and Cox—split the profits generated by their prostitutes. On the night of Gabel's murder, Cox was near Gabel's bar, shuffling the schedules of the street cops so that none were around when the gunmen opened fire. Two months later Cox was implicated in Looney's auto theft ring; he was suspended from duty and later resigned altogether. By the end of the year, Cox had been charged with an impressive range of crimes, including auto theft and murder, but he died in October 1924, before his case ever made it to trial.

It was left to a newspaper to go after Looney. The *Argus* began an aggressive campaign, speaking for all of Rock Island in expressing outrage over Gabel's murder. They published an editorial that read:

"The thing for you to keep in mind, Mr. Good Citizen, is that the murder of Bill Gabel was unwritten notice to you and the other 35,000 residents of Rock Island that the price of interference with the activities of the local underworld is death. And that threat will remain over your head just so long as you continue to tolerate the present vicious condition in your city. Rock Island belongs to you, not to the band of itinerant thugs and prostitutes."

The *Argus* didn't let up after that, publishing stinging editorials day after day until Looney's empire finally ended with a dramatic collapse on October 6, 1922, the day of the Market Street shootout. On an unusually warm fall afternoon—it was 88 degrees—hundreds of people had gathered on the streets of downtown Rock Island to watch the scoreboard in front of the *Argus'* office; they were following updates from game 3 of the World Series between the New York Giants and the New York Yankees.

Looney and his son, Connor, pulled up to the Sherman Hotel, followed closely by Lawrence Pedigo, who ran the hotel. Right after they parked, two cars raced up and parked opposite them. Several men got out of the car and opened fire on the group. Connor was hit right away and fell in the street, while the others ran into the hotel for cover. Bystander Albert J. Allguyer, a visitor from Brooklyn, started walking toward Connor, maybe to help, maybe out of confusion, but he was knocked to the ground when a bullet pierced his gut. Looney and Pedigo started firing back from the second floor of the hotel, spraying bullets up and down Market Street and motivating the large crowd to scatter. Shots were fired from what seemed like everywhere—hotel windows shattered, bullets chipped off pieces of bricks on the storefronts. The men that started the attack got back in their cars when they ran out of ammo and sped off down Third Avenue with the police right behind them. The gunmen were later identified as Dan Drost and Anthony Billburg—two former Looney allies—and Jake Ramser, a long-time enemy.

Allguyer, the bystander from Brooklyn, survived. Connor wasn't so lucky. He died at St. Anthony Hospital about eight hours after being shot; multiple bullets had ripped apart his body. He was just 21. Although no one from Looney's side was charged, the *Argus* wasn't about to let anyone forget the underlying cause. In the story about the shootout, they asked readers "Who killed Bill Gabel?"

In his testimony to the Grand Jury a few weeks later, Billburg claimed the whole thing had been planned by prominent members of the community to get rid of John Looney, stalwarts like Jake Ramser, John Potter (publisher of the *Argus*), and John Colligan (managing editor of the *Argus*). Billburg claimed that he was promised immunity, that no one would go to jail for the shootings. The evidence pointed to Billburg as the one who organized the whole thing, but the details didn't add up. Should we really be surprised if those community leaders had had enough of Looney and wanted to be rid of him for good? His death was the surest way to make that happen.

In the wake of the Market Street shootout, nine more people were killed, including James "Dude" Brown, a well-known gambler who was shot after being caught dealing from the bottom of the deck, or at least that was the cover story. It's more likely that Looney foreclosed on his life, because Brown had fallen behind in his debt payments. The rash of killings forced Mayor Schriver to crack down; he ordered the closure of all the bars and brothels in Rock Island's red light district. Three days after the shootout, the Illinois Attorney General opened an investigation into the murder of Bill Gabel and the next day, Tuesday, October 10, twenty-five government agents descended on Rock Island and began rifling through records. Looney buried Connor then fled, first to Ottawa, then to Denver, then to New Mexico. By the time he reached his ranch, he had been indicted in federal court for auto theft. The legal system was about to lower Looney's rank in the food chain.

Back in my room, Jefferson and I were trying to piece together the Starck family history. "So Bill Gabel left behind at least one child, a son named Jerry Gabel, who later became a Starck?"

"That's right. Gabel's wife, Vivian , later remarried Steve Starck; he's the one who adopted Jerry," I said.

"So Agent William Starck's grandfather was orphaned, maybe that's not the right word but you know what I mean, was orphaned by John Looney."

"Right. Orphaned."

"That's interesting, Frank, but I'm not sure yet how it helps us here. I still say we need to keep Agent Starck on our side; we don't need to be pissing him off."

"I understand. I just think there's more going on with him than he lets on. Maybe it won't help us solve Miguel's murder, but, at the very least, he may have a story that I can write about. I've been looking for a contemporary connection to Looney, right? That's why I came here. I thought Miguel was going to be my story, but maybe I have a new one to follow."

"Just don't let it get in the way of clearing your name here. Don't go pissing him off. Promise?"

"Yeah. I promise." I figured there was a lot of work I could do to get to the Starck family history without anyone knowing, without pissing him off.

"Why do I get the feeling that you're not going to let this go? Anyway, let me tell you what happened when I went back to the Crooked Spine tonight."

27

I pulled the shades closed in my room and flipped on the lights. It was getting dark outside, and I didn't want to invite every other motel guest to look in my room. Jefferson was standing near the front door.

"I went back to the Crooked Spine at 7," he began. "It was busier than Sunday night, but I still found a seat at the end of the bar. Noah was popping a couple of Miller Lites, but he nodded in my direction as I sat down."

****

"Beam on the rocks?" Noah asked as he slid a couple of beer cans across bar.

"Sure. A little busier tonight." He walked over and put the glass in front of me.

"How's your vacation coming along?"

"Not too bad. Got to sleep in today. That was nice. How about you? Working nights must be tough."

"Not for me. I'm a night person. I don't mind working here 'til 1 or 2, 'cause I'm gonna be awake for a while longer anyway. I don't usually go to sleep until 4 or 5."

"What do you do at that time of night? Seems like there's not much going on around here that late."

"I just hang out at home or with friends. Sometimes I go fishing. Not much competition that time of night for a good spot."

"I suppose not." Noah excused himself to take care of a couple of customers. He stopped in the middle of the bar and handed a beer to a guy who I hadn't noticed earlier. Even with a hoodie drawn around his head, I could tell it was Cody. When the Moline PD brought him in, I watched the interrogation from the right side of the two-way mirror; he was wearing the same sweatshirt that day (on the back it said "I got 99 problems but a snitch ain't one"). Noah leaned in and said something to Cody, who nodded once and turned his head slightly in my direction. I got up to use the bathroom, and when I came back, Cody was sitting on a stool next to mine, looking at his phone.

"What's up?" I said, turning to face him, then looking back in Noah's direction.

"Not much. Just having a couple of beers." Cody took a sip of Stag without lifting his gaze from the phone.

"They have plenty of that here. Guess you're in the right place."

"Yeah, guess I am. I haven't seen you here before. Where you from?"

I told him I was from Chicago and checked the urge to make fun of the way he kept playing with his phone.

"I love it there, a real badass town," Cody said, finally looking up. "What part of Chicago are you from?"

"South side."

"You must be a Sox fan."

"Never really got into baseball, but don't get me started on the Bears. How about you? You follow any sports?"

"I'm a Cubs fan, so no. Southside is pretty rough

from what I hear, kinda wide open, lots of gangs and drugs and shit like that. I bet you have to watch your back all the time." Cody did something with his hands as he talked; maybe he thought he was flashing gang signs, but he looked more like an interpreter for the deaf having a seizure.

"Some parts are rough and some are fine. Just depends on where you are." I emptied my glass of Beam and set the glass back down on the bar. "I can take care of myself, though. Sounds like this little area can be rough, too. The bartender told me one of the customers here was just killed, a Mexican dude, I think he said."

"Yeah. We've got our bad areas, too."

"Someone you knew?"

"You could say that."

"Sorry to hear about it."

"Don't be sorry. You know what they say: you get what you sow." Cody used his hand to simulate a gun firing.

Noah poured me a refill. I turned to Cody and in my best Samuel Jackson voice said: "Be not deceived. God is not mocked: for whatsoever a man soweth, that shall he also reap. For he that soweth to his flesh shall of the flesh reap corruption; but he that soweth to the Spirit shall of the Spirit reap life everlasting." I took a sip of the whiskey, letting it linger on my tongue as my words bounced around inside Cody's head. "One of my favorite Bible quotes there; Galatians 6, verses 7 and 8. A lot of wisdom in those short verses."

"So that's where that comes from." Cody fidgeted in his chair, then changed the subject. "So what kinda work do you do?"

"Insurance," I told him.

"Insurance, huh?" Cody looked back down at his phone, scrolling through pages of something, probably his Facebook news feed. "I guess that could be interesting work, depending upon what you're insuring."

"I like what I do. I'm my own boss, mostly, and the pay's pretty good. Someone always needs insurance for something, you know? They feel better when they have a little more protection from the bad things that can fuck up your life, and your business." By now, I was pretty sure that Cody was having a hard time reading me. I wanted him to wonder if I was just a new face looking to buy a little weed from him, or if this guy from Chicago, this black guy, might have a different agenda, like trying to make a dent in his business.

"What brings a Chicago guy who sells insurance to the Quad Cities?" Cody put down the phone and started working on his beer again.

"I needed a little get away, so I came here to visit a friend for a few days and to check out the scene."

"I can think of better places to go than here, places with a better scene."

"It seems fine to me, maybe a little quiet for my tastes, but quiet can be good, too."

"We've got plenty of quiet, most of the time. Is there anything you want to know about the QCA, something I can help you with, so you enjoy your getaway more?"

I turned to look at him, like I was giving him a good top-to-bottom inspection, then told him: "I like a lot of things. Tonight I have a taste for something to help me chill. I thought a couple of shots of Beam would do it, but I feel like I'm going to need something else to me mellow out."

"Like what exactly? A yoga class? Michael Bolton?"

"Something that's less work and that doesn't kill my desire to go on living, maybe something herbal."

"I wish I could help you, dude, but I'm not into that scene. Have you talked to the bartender? Maybe he knows someone."

"Yeah. He told me that he knows someone who might help. Thought that might be you, but hey, it's no big deal. I just thought it might help me relax."

"Well, good luck with that. I gotta get going. Hope you find what you're looking for." Cody finished his beer and left. The crowd was thinning out; happy hour was over and no one had come in for dinner. Noah wiped down the bar, working his way toward me.

"You still looking for a little something extra to help your mood tonight, buddy?"

"Sure am."

"I got you covered, just this one time. It's not my thing, selling it, you know, but I'd be rude if I didn't help out a visitor, right?" Noah said without looking up. He reached into a pocket and slid a plastic bag in my direction. "That's two grams. It's yours for $20."

****

"I paid him for the pot, settled my tab, and left. Cody obviously didn't want to sell to me directly; didn't trust me, I guess. I can't say I blame him."

"So what are you going to do with the pot?" I asked.

"It's evidence now, Frank. I'll be passing it along to the Moline PD."

"Just asking. It's such a small amount after all; it can't really help the investigation that much, seems to me."

"Damn it, Frank. It's evidence; drop it."

"You used to be more fun."

"You used to be more responsible. Look, I'm tired. It's been a long day. Let's put this to rest for now." He turned around and walked out of the room.

28

Since coming clean about everything that happened Friday night I felt better, relieved mostly, but I was worried about Jefferson, about what he thought of me. Sure, he was trying to act like everything was OK, that we'd figure a way out of this mess. But I knew he was disappointed in me, and I hated that.

We'd been through a lot since we'd known each other, but I always felt like he was on my side, even when I did something stupid, which, if you listened to Jefferson, happened all the time. After telling him about Friday night, I wasn't so sure. I knew he disapproved of what I did that night. That's nothing new. This time, though, I made some stupid decisions and someone ended up dead. I was afraid that he was beginning to re-evaluate the nature of our friendship, maybe feeling like I had become too much of a drag on his life. I knew he'd go all out to help me, but, for the first time since I'd known him, I wasn't sure if we'd still be talking after that.

Sitting in my motel room alone, I was feeling restless and confined, so I went back to the Diving Duck in search of some breathing room. When I got there, Marge and Becca occupied one end of the bar, with several empty stools nearby. I sat down and took a sip of the coffee stout that had just appeared in front of me.

"Hey, Pops."

"Welcome back, Frank," He reached out to shake my hand. "How's it going? Found any good stories?"

At least Pops was happy to see me. "One or two, I suppose," was all I could muster.

"Geez, you look wiped out," Marge observed. "You need to slow down and smell the hops, or in your case, the malt."

"Exactly what I'm trying to do." I let the first sip linger in my mouth; a little malty up front, a hint of chocolate, followed by an explosion of coffee flavor. "Perfect," I said. Pops smiled and walked away to pour a couple more pints.

"How well do you know your local history?" I asked Marge and Becca.

"I stay on top of things pretty well," Marge said.

"Have you heard of a family named Starck; some of them were cops?"

"Starck. That name is vaguely familiar," Marge said. "If I'm thinking of the right family, aren't they more Moline than Rock Island?" she asked as she turned to Becca. "Didn't one of them get in trouble for something?"

"Don't look at me," Becca answered. "I've never heard of them."

I jumped in to help out. "You're on the right track, Marge. One of the Starcks shot and killed a guy who was accused of child abuse."

"Right. I kinda remember that, but not too well. It must have been a while ago. Why are you interested in them, Frank?"

"I've been following the story about the kid whose body was found in Suiter Slough. There's an FBI guy who's investigating it whose name is Starck. I thought I remembered hearing something about his father."

"How the heck did you get involved in that?" Marge asked.

"I'm still trying to figure that out. The kid who died was named Miguel Ramirez. He moved up here from Texas to go to Dickey. I met him and his roommate, Cody Hahn, when I first got in town."

"Cody Hahn? I know that kid," Becca said, her head snapping toward me. "We went to college together." She folded her arms and turned back to the bar. "I hated him."

"Why?" I wondered. "What was so awful about him?"

"He's a total jerk. Pretty as God, but what a jerk. So full of himself. I tried to get to know him. Honestly? I wanted to nail him, so I sat next to him in an econ class, but I had a hard time just getting him to acknowledge that I existed, at least until he needed a copy of my notes. He wasn't popular; most people didn't like him, but everyone knew him, and I mean everyone. That seemed suspicious, so I figured he must be selling drugs."

"Drugs, huh? That seems like a leap. Was that just a rumor or did you have reason to believe he really was dealing?"

"I never bought anything from him, but there was one night he showed up at my apartment. Nobody told me he was coming over, and he didn't stay long. I'm pretty sure that I saw my roommate give him cash, and, a few minutes later she was lighting up a bong. I think that's pretty good evidence. Don't you?"

"Sure. What else do you know about him?"

"He was kinda dumb," Becca said, unable to stop herself from laughing. "I know he didn't get good grades. I don't know how he graduated at all. What really got to me is that he always acted like the world owed him something, you know? I was supposed to give him my class notes because he was pretty or something, but he wouldn't talk to me in public because I wasn't special enough for him? What a jerk. Then somehow he got in Dickey. I didn't see that coming. He'll probably finish last in his class, if he graduates at all."

We switched to lighter topics after that, whether the coffee stout was too coffee-ish, whether Justin Bieber or Maroon 5 was more dreadful, that kind of thing, drinking a couple more beers before I called it a night.

I had trouble falling asleep; I was trying to process what I knew about Cody. He was an asshole; I already knew that, and a drug dealer, too, or, more specifically, a pot dealer. Did Cody know that Miguel was also selling drugs? Could Cody have killed Miguel because of a dispute over their respective dealings? That could be a motive, but the last time I saw Cody, when Miguel helped him out of the Locked Down, he was barely conscious, knocked down by the alcohol and my punches, mostly my punches. I find it hard to believe that he got himself sober enough to be at Suiter Park just three hours later and together enough to kill Miguel. On the other hand, he and Noah seemed tight, and Jefferson followed Noah to Suiter Park the other night. Maybe the two of them, Cody and Noah, worked something out to get rid of Miguel.

I also couldn't stop thinking about the day's other big news: the link between Agent Starck and Bill Gabel. Honestly, I've never been one who believed that the sins of the ancestors had to defile the whole family. Agent Starck is his own man and shouldn't be judged by the actions of his father and grandfather. Right? More to the point, was this my new story, the one that I could salvage from this trip? Will Agent Starck talk to me about his family history? And if I write about the Starcks and their ties to a long dead gangster, can I find someone to publish it?

29

Whatever sleep I managed to get was cut short by the sunlight leaking into my room. Cheap rooms come with thin shades. Once I convinced myself to roll out of bed, I lingered in the shower, still trying to connect pot, Cody and Noah, and crooked cops. I found some reasonably clean clothes, freshened them up with a generous spray of Febreze before putting them on, and walked over to Donna's Diner to meet Jefferson for breakfast.

"You wouldn't have been able to do anything, Frank." Jefferson said, not wasting time with small talk this morning. "You couldn't have rescued Miguel." He emptied sugar into his cup as he talked, barely looking up at me.

"What makes you so sure?"

"Look. You're a therapist turned travel writer. You're not a cop. You never served in the military; hell, you never even took a self-defense class, for all I know. You can throw a good punch at a kid who's had too much to drink, but you're basically a…"

"A what?"

"…a pussy."

I was surprised by his comment and more than a little hurt. I picked up a menu to hide behind.

"Oh, don't go cowering on me. You know it's true. It was true when we were in school, and I had to bail you out every time you got picked on, and it's still true today. You're good with words, real good, but you're not good with your fists," he said, clenching his right hand for emphasis. "Look. The point is that, even if you tried to do something to help, you probably would have fucked it up. You would have put yourself in more danger. Hell, you might have fucking drowned. For once, you actually made the right call."

"I can swim," I said, without lifting my eyes from the menu.

Jefferson lowered his voice. "Like you said, the killer was probably still there, and he would not have been happy to see you. You would've ended up in the same place that Miguel did, and I'd be up here pissed off, trying to figure out who killed my best friend."

At least he still considered me his best friend. I put the menu down and looked at him.

"Can we get back to the big picture here?" Jefferson continued. "You are still a suspect in the murder, and you were at the scene of the crime probably just minutes before Miguel was killed. You haven't leveled with law enforcement about everything you did that night, which isn't going to look good when they get the truth—which they will—plus you used a fake Facebook profile to track Miguel before you met him, which makes you look even more suspicious. I can see why the cops would be interested in you. You've dug one hell of a hole."

"When you put it that way, it sounds like I'm screwed." Our server, Ashley again, came by and took our orders.

"On the other hand, they don't' have any physical evidence to tie you to the murder. They haven't even come up with a good reason that you might have wanted to kill Miguel. That's the only thing that's kept you from getting locked up so far. No motive. But it looks like there are other people who might have had a motive to kill Miguel. How about Cody? Could he have done it? He had a motive, or it's easy to imagine one. He was blackmailing Miguel. Maybe Miguel had had enough and was ready to cut him loose. Maybe that's why Cody was acting so aggressive that night."

"I don't know. It doesn't seem likely. I mean, the guy was out cold after I hit him."

"I think it's safe to assume that he bounced back quickly; I remember how you punch."

"Ouch. OK. So let's say it was Cody. Besides the blackmailing, he and Miguel were both selling pot. Did they know that? Maybe Cody had just found out about Miguel's dealing and was pissed. But how did Cody get Miguel to Suiter Park? They live together, for Christ's sake, so what could Cody say to get Miguel there so late?"

"Maybe Miguel wasn't really dealing, or not dealing much. Maybe he took some of Cody's stash to sell for a little extra cash. That might be why he was willing to share some of the profits with you, to cover your gambling losses. So then Cody figured out that Miguel had stolen from him and set up a meeting at the island to collect. He would have still been drunk, so maybe he wasn't thinking very clearly, and, based on what you told me earlier, he was impulsive, maybe impulsive enough to hit Miguel in the head if he was pissed off."

"I don't know. Something about it doesn't seem right to me," I said. "I just don't see why they had to go to Suiter Park for that."

"OK. What if Noah sent the message, not Cody. Noah's not clean in this whole thing. I know it. It looks like he and Cody are pretty tight, so maybe they worked together. Neither one of them seems bothered by Miguel's death. I'd almost go so far as to say they are downright gleeful about it. Besides that, I saw Noah going to Suiter Park really late. He likes to fish at night, so maybe that's how he got Miguel down there. He was there fishing, anyway."

Ashley returned with our food. "Good. I'm starving," I said. "So Noah sent a message to Miguel, maybe saying he wanted to buy from him? If Cody had passed out and Noah couldn't reach him after work, he might be looking for someone else to restock his stash. So, maybe it was just Noah, then?"

"I guess that's another possibility. Noah also told me that he was pissed off when Miguel raised the price of the pot that Noah was trying to buy."

"It's also safe to say that Noah doesn't like Mexicans too much. Maybe he was out to get rid of one."

"I don't really see that, Frank. Look, I know Noah made some comments that sounded racist, but this was personal. He had something against Miguel; all that shit he said about Mexicans was really just meant for Miguel. At least that's what it looks like to me now. If we go to his place and find a closet full of white linens, I could change my mind."

"You may be right, but I still think his favorite color is white, as white as this plate is going to be after I wipe up the egg yolk with this toast," I said, holding up a slice of bread and shaking it.

"Take it easy, Frank. I guess it's also possible Noah and Cody worked together to pull this off. Anyway, at least we have some ideas. If we're really going to get this figured out, though, it's time for you to 'fess up. We need to go to the Moline police, and you need to tell them the whole story. The whole story, Frank. They're gonna find out anyway; better they hear it from you now."

I knew Jefferson was right, but I was having a hard time convincing myself to take that step. I'm not going to look good. I've lied about a few important details, like gambling with Miguel in the casino, finding his body in the slough and running away, the possible drug deal to get back money I lost at the casino, that kind of thing. Maybe I could leave out the drug deal. If they find out about the details of that night on their own, though, I won't just look bad, I'll look like a criminal trying to cover his tracks. "You're right," I said. "Let's go and get this over with."

30

Good intentions don't count for much when you've lied to the people who have the keys to freedom strapped to their belts, an insight I began to appreciate as the Moline cops cuffed me and threw me in a cell. They weren't amused at the details I'd omitted from our previous conversations. Jefferson didn't look all that surprised when they took me away.

"Hang in there, buddy," he called out to me, shrugging his shoulders as the cops pulled me out of the interrogation room and toward a night of confinement. "Hang in there. I'll get you out in no time."

****

That wasn't my first time in jail, although the accommodations in Moline were a little nicer than in Colombia. After my trek through Panama's Darién Gap, we crossed the border into Colombia and found our way to Capurganá, an idyllic city on the southwestern edge of the Caribbean Sea with no road connections to the rest of the world. The city was isolated, but they did have an immigration office.

I was feeling great. I had just survived a trek through the infamous isthmus—the impenetrable Darién Gap!—even if the guides I hired—two Panamanians and two

Colombians, you can't be too careful—did most of the work. We packed very little gear so we could stay mobile enough to flee with little notice, if such a need were to arise, which it did a couple of times. The dense, mountainous rain forest is a great place to hide if you don't want to be found, so the bandits are a bigger threat than the jaguars and the malaria. I was pretty good with a compass and taking notes and the accidental humor that comes from being clumsy, so that was pretty much my role—cartographer/diarist/jester. At least I knew how to get out of their way and let them do the work I hired them to do.

Once we checked in at Capurganá , it didn't take long for the immigration officials to sour my mood. We walked into a drab concrete block building at the port. It was a warm day but inside the office it was suffocating. The lone fan, an ancient steel model that sat in a corner behind the desk, squeaked and whirred as it circulated stale air, twisting from one side to the other. Maybe the two immigration officers were just grumpy from the heat, but when we presented our papers and told them where we had just come from, they frowned and began yelling at us. We knew the authorities actively discouraged tourists from making that trek—they didn't want the hassle and expense of trying to rescue Western tourists—but we didn't think we were breaking any laws by doing it. The two immigration officers spent about half an hour looking at each other and flipping through photocopied pages in a three-ring binder, certain that we must have broken some law, so they threw us in jail on suspicion of being suspicious, at least that's how I translated their

Spanish.

Capurganá may be a lovely tropical city, but the jail didn't have the amenities of a standard Caribbean resort. My cell was dark—not a view of the sea to be found— and the floor was a mix of dirt and decaying concrete. It was musty and hot and reeked of urine, probably from the small plastic bucket in one corner that was filled with the excrement and piss of previous guests. When I wasn't lightheaded from dehydration, I felt nauseous from the smells. Every couple of days, a guy in a uniform would show up with a hose and give me a shower. At least I had a cell to myself, unlike my guides—the benefits of US citizenship!—who were all tossed in a dorm with a couple dozen of other suspicious suspects.

A couple of times a day, someone would show up with a plate of food, usually plantains and red beans. Other than the person who hosed me and delivered the food, I never saw anyone else. No guards looked in on me, no lawyers came to consult, no visits from the US embassy. After surviving a daring trek through a remote part of the world, I was beginning to think that I was going to wither away in a dark jail cell, forgotten, never to be heard from again.

The longer I was stuck in that cell, the more I wondered who might miss me, if I died in that Colombian jail. The list surprised me, mostly because it was so short: Jefferson, for sure; Anna Hanks, my mentor, yes; my brother, probably; a couple of friends from college, I think so; the therapists I worked with, not at all. If I'd died ten years earlier, my memorial service could have filled a church, or at least a decent-sized chapel. If I'd died in Colombia, though, my family could have saved a lot of money and just had a quick graveside service.

Sitting in that cell, for the first time since I quit my job and hit the road, I was beginning to feel worn out. Instead of being excited by the novelty of visiting new places, I grew weary of feeling foreign. I was ready to return to the US, to start building a new life. But what would I do when I got there (if I got there)? Going back to my old life wasn't an option. And, just because I wanted to go back to the States didn't mean I was ready to stop traveling. Not at all. Assuming I got out of that stinking jail, I wanted to get to know my home better. I didn't know it when I was sitting in that cell, but a few days after getting back to St. Louis, I would realize that my home wasn't one specific place, it wasn't a house on a block that had been surveyed and numbered so Google maps could tell you exactly how to get there. No; my home, I would realize, wasn't that fixed. It was anywhere along the Mississippi River.

After a week in that Colombian jail, a woman from immigration showed up with a guard who opened the cell door. I was told that I was no longer considered suspicious and given an entry stamp and 30 days to enjoy the country. Welcome to Colombia! I wouldn't use a single one of those days. The men who guided me through the Darién Gap were released at the same time. They seemed to take incarceration in stride, much more so than I did, joking about feeling relaxed after a week of rest. I just felt spent. I thanked them, tipped them a little extra, and we said adios. I went right from the jail to the airport and booked a flight to an unknown life in a familiar place. After a two-week jungle trek and a week on an involuntary diet, I had lost some 30 pounds. I'd have to buy some new clothes when I got back to St. Louis.

At least the Moline jail had a bed with some cushion and a real toilet, and I was pretty sure I wouldn't be stuck eating plantains and red beans again. And while I was on my own in that Colombian jail, I wasn't in Moline. I knew Jefferson was looking out for me.

****

As I told the full story about my night with Miguel to Detective Martens, he got increasingly irritated. They hadn't yet discovered that Miguel met me at the casino later that night, and, while they suspected I saw more of the island than I let on, they sure didn't know why. Now that I had told them everything, maybe they would figure out who did it, or maybe, I suppose, they could focus on me even more intensely. The thing is, when Martens cuffed me, he was obviously pissed, but he didn't tell me that I was being charged with anything, he just threw me in jail. And, I was pretty sure I saw a grin break out on his face as he closed the cell door.

Maybe the cops just needed a little time to cool off, a little time for my story to fully sink in. Maybe they wanted a little longer to look for holes in what I told them. At least I wasn't hiding anything anymore. When I talked to them again, I wouldn't have to keep track of any new lies or omissions. One thing that struck me as funny was that they didn't seem to care at all about the reason I came to the Quad Cities in the first place, to track down a descendant of John Looney. I should have been arrested in Rock Island, I guess.

What did manage to get their attention was the drug deal gone bad, that and the part about me seeing Miguel's body in the water and not reporting it. They were very interested in those two details. Cody had already told them that Miguel had been in trouble for running drugs, but they weren't inclined to believe him. Now that I'd told the same story—and of Cody's alleged dealing— they were much more interested in the drug angle. Maybe it really was just a dispute over drugs.

31

The next morning, Detective Martens escorted me from my cell to that familiar interrogation room. I sat at the table under the florescent light, opposite what I assumed was a two-way mirror. The detective stood across from me, hands on the table and leaning in toward me. As he spoke, he shared his breakfast with me, the scent of bacon and coffee still strong on his breath.

"We're not going to charge you with anything," he began. "Yet."

"Does that mean I can go?"

"Soon. We're still confused about a few details in your story. Tell me again about the text Miguel sent you, after you dropped him off at Suiter Park. How long after he went into the park did he send it?"

"I got it awhile after I dropped him off, maybe 30 minutes."

"And what did he ask you to do?"

"He said he left his backpack in the car and asked me to bring it to him. After I said I'd do it, he sent me another text with directions about how to find him."

"What was in the backpack?"

"I have no idea. I didn't open it." I don't know why, but I felt stupid telling him that, like if I had been a little more curious and opened that backpack, I might have figured out sooner that something was rotten.

"OK. So you grabbed the backpack and went onto the island. How long did it take you to get from your car to the spot where you found his body?"

"I'm not really sure, but I can guess. I walked slowly, constantly looking around. I didn't want to get jumped by anyone when I was trying to find Miguel. It probably wasn't too long, maybe 10 or 15 minutes."

"So sometime during those 10 or 15 minutes, someone found Miguel, hit him in the head, and threw his body in the water? That's a very efficient criminal." I don't think he approved of my timeline.

"I guess so. He sent me a text just a few minutes earlier, so it must have happened during that time. I guess."

"What did you do with the backpack?"

"I dropped it when I saw his body floating in the water. I guess I left it behind."

"You guess?"

"I don't specifically remember leaving it behind—I was a little freaked out at the time, you know? But I don't have it now. So, yes, I guess that means I left it on the island. It should have been near the spot where I saw his body."

The detective stood up and paced a few steps before turning back to face me. "Look, Dodge, I tend to believe your story, your latest story. At least I do right now. But I'm bothered by a couple of things. We don't have any physical evidence, no phone—I suppose it could have fallen into the water, but it wasn't on his body—no backpack, no drugs, no blunt object that could have been used to hit him in the head. I suppose the killer could have come back to retrieve all those things, but I'd feel a lot better if we could find something. You said you didn't see anyone else around there, right?"

"That's right. I didn't see anyone. But it was raining pretty hard by the time I left, so I couldn't really see very much around me, anyway. My car was the only one in the parking lot, though, when I got there and when I left."

The detective had heard enough at that point, so he let me go. I called Jefferson for a ride and an update.

"How was your night in jail?" he teased me as I got into his car.

"Uncomfortable. Thanks for asking."

"They just wanted to send you a message, to let you know that you shouldn't have lied to them, that you should have told them everything up front. I thought it was a good idea, too." Jefferson was upbeat and smiling.

"Thanks, I suppose," I said. "Hey, are you saying you knew they were going to throw me in jail before we got there?"

"It was only for one night, Frank. I thought it might do you some good, give you some time to chill out and reflect. I know how you much you like to reflect."

"So you and the detective worked that out in advance. I'm not sure what to think of that."

"Don't. Martens is an old friend; we went to the academy together. Don't get all worked up over it.

The good news is that I think your confession worked. I'm pretty sure they believe you now, and you're not a suspect anymore. They're on your side now. I had some time to chat with them about the whole case, too. We still have two angles we're pursuing. We think there's a good chance that Cody and Noah worked together to kill Miguel. We'd also like to ask Agent Starck a few more questions about his role in all of this, but he's a very hard man to reach. So we turned up the volume a little, to get his attention. Take a look at this."

Jefferson handed me a copy of that day's *Moline Herald*. "Turn to page two," he told me.

10 Years Ago

Moline Detective Leo Starck shot and killed 52-year old Andrew Wriedt, who was wanted for child molestation. Starck, who was alone when he attempted to arrest Wriedt, claimed self-defense. According to anonymous sources, an internal investigation concluded that Starck went to Wriedt's house with the intention of killing him. No charges were filed but Starck resigned from the police department, with his benefits and pension intact. Starck's father, Jerry, was a police officer in Rock Island who was also forced to resign under a cloud of suspicion after a series of suspects in his custody died. Corruption ran in the family. All are descendants of Bill Gabel, a former Rock Island police officer who turned in his badge to sell bootleg liquor for the notorious gangster, John Looney. Compiled by Steve DeSmet

32

Jefferson took me to Donna's Diner for breakfast and to catch me up.

"After you were thrown in jail, Detective Martens brought Cody in for questioning and searched his apartment. They didn't find any drugs or evidence that would tie him to Miguel's death, which is no surprise; Cody had time to clean the place up after Miguel died. The police had searched the apartment after Miguel's death, but they only searched Miguel's room and the common areas because they didn't see Cody as a suspect. They took him to the station but he didn't have much to say, so they locked him up, too. He might have been just a couple of cells down from you, in fact."

"Too bad I didn't know. We could have bonded by comparing the amenities of our cells."

"They tried to find Noah yesterday, too, but he disappeared. Couldn't find him at home, either. He was scheduled for a couple days off from work, but I suspect he was tipped off, by Cody, that the cops might come looking for him. Imagine the great time you would have had if all three of you had been locked up in Moline."

"A guy can dream."

"At least all of you would have been out of our way for a while. While the Moline cops were busy with you and Cody, I decided to do a little more work on Noah.

I checked his record and called the sheriff down where he used to live. Turns out that Noah had some trouble at home. He had a couple of arrests for possession, small amounts of weed, and got busted a couple of times for illegal trapping or catching too many fish, but nothing really stuck. Before the flood, he was a bartender at the strip club. Made a few enemies because he had to break up a couple of fights and sometimes had to get between a handsy customer and one of the girls. His sister got a job there, waiting tables but hoping to land a job on the stage. A couple of guys got too friendly with her one night, and Noah got really pissed. Didn't just kick them out, but made sure he punched them a few times first. Just for good measure, he followed the guys out of the bar and beat them with a baseball bat. They survived, but Noah did a few months in the county jail for assault. That's why he moved away. He got fired and had to pay restitution for the assaults; he probably didn't have any money left to rebuild his house."

"Did the sheriff say anything about Noah's affection for Mexicans?"

"Not directly. I don't think the sheriff is too fond of Spanish-speaking folks himself, but he did mention that one of the guys Noah beat up was Mexican. The victims were both from Fort Madison, in Iowa."

"Yeah, that's just across the Mississippi from Niota."

"Well, both were from there, born there, in fact, which means they were both Americans, just one was Mexican American."

"I'm not surprised. The railroad recruited workers to Fort Madison from Mexico during World War I, so

219

there have been Mexican and Mexican American families there for nearly 100 years."

"So we still gotta find Noah. We've got a couple of cops out knocking on doors and checking places we know he frequented, but I'd feel better if we had him in custody, too. I don't like the idea of him running around free."

33

We paid up at the diner and went back to the motel.

"So how do you think Agent Starck fits into all this?" I asked.

"I'm not really sure, but it's funny how Starck's name keeps coming up. He's the one who tipped me off about Miguel. He was using Miguel as an informant. He just happened to be in the Quad Cities when Miguel died. Hell, maybe he killed Miguel, although I don't know what his motive would be. On the other hand, look at that family he comes from: one fuckin' crooked cop after another. We also found out that Starck is supposed to be on vacation right now. He wasn't calling me back when I called his cell, so we finally got an office number to call. They said he'd been away from the office for about a week, went home to visit family for a few days. So he just happened to be home in the Quad Cities when Miguel was killed? Something smells fishy about that. I think he had something else going on with Miguel, something outside of work," Jefferson said.

"Like what?"

Jefferson stopped in front of the door to his room. "This is a wild guess, but, what the hell. He arrested Miguel for running drugs, right? Got him to give up some names and details. We also know that Miguel was still doing some dealing and didn't seem worried about getting caught. So what if Miguel wasn't dipping into Cody's stash? What if he and Starck were somehow working together? Starck might have to come up here from time to time to collect his share and keep Miguel accountable. I don't know where Miguel's murder fits in with this, but it might explain Starck's involvement and why he's been so reluctant to return our phone calls."

"He seems suspicious to me," I said. "But how do you go about investigating an FBI agent?"

"Very quietly. You start by not telling the FBI about it. We have a couple of ideas. For one thing, we're going back to look more closely at his father and grandfather."

"What can I do to help?"

"Take a shower. You stink. Then maybe you can use some of those magic research skills you have and see what you can find out about the guys who were killed by the Starcks."

Jefferson may have been right about the benefits of a night in jail. I don't normally take well to being ordered around, but that time I did exactly what Jefferson told me to do. After I cleaned up, I headed over to the Rock Island County Historical Society and started digging through their files.

I started with Steve Wriedt, the guy killed by Agent Starck's father, Leo. There wasn't much to like about Wriedt. He was 52 years old when Leo Starck killed him, and he'd spent half of his adult life in prison, mostly for assaults and robberies. He was released from prison just six months before he was killed. The police got an anonymous tip that Wriedt had molested a 12-year-old girl in his neighborhood. Leo Starck managed to be the first one on the scene. According to the newspaper account, Leo entered the home after clearly identifying himself as a police officer. The suspect came running out of the kitchen and charged at Officer Starck with a butcher's knife. Leo said he reacted instinctively, by pulling out his gun and firing until Wriedt fell to the ground, putting four bullets in his chest in just a couple of seconds.

I was curious about Steve Wriedt's family, so I looked up his parents, Thomas Wriedt and Angela Schneiderhorst. I didn't find out much about his mother, but his father worked for John Deere for most of his life; Thomas Wriedt was 69 years old when he died in 1991. I kept digging and found a birth certificate for Thomas. I let out an audible "wow" when I read that his mother was Helen Van Dale, the infamous queen of prostitution who worked closely with John Looney; his father was listed as unknown. Van Dale was married to Eddie Wriedt but not until two years after Thomas was born. In 1922, she would have still been involved with Police Chief Tom Cox, who died in 1924. Eddie Wriedt died in 1925, just a year after marrying Van Dale. Being involved with Van Dale wasn't good for a man's health.

The evidence was all circumstantial, but I was convinced that Thomas Wriedt's father was actually Tom Cox, the former police chief who was in Looney's pocket, and that Eddie Wriedt had adopted him after marrying Van Dale. Tom Cox. Another Looney collaborator. Leo Starck killed a man who was probably the grandson of the corrupt police chief that worked for John Looney.

I kept digging. Leo Starck's father was Jerry. I already knew that he was Bill Gabel's son. Jerry served in the

Army in World War II in the Military Police Corps. He was hired by the Moline Police Department to work as a guard in the jail after getting home from the war, but he didn't make a career of police work; he resigned in 1959. The *Argus* printed a short article about his departure, suggesting that he had been negligent in the deaths of four men who had died on his watch; the article didn't include the names of the dead inmates, though. After he resigned, he worked as a private security guard for a few companies until a heart attack killed him in 1973. I searched through a few more articles but still couldn't find the names of any of the men who died while in Leo Starck's custody. Time to call Jefferson.

"Hey, Brian. You having any luck?"

"Yeah. I got a look at the police report for the Steve Wreidt shooting. I don't think everything's in there, but it looks like they ruled out self-defense. Frank, I'd bet that they believed Leo Starck killed Wriedt without provocation. The file has an interview with one of Wriedt's relatives that makes it sound like the two men knew each other. I don't know if Leo Starck had arrested him before or what, but that might be worth following up on."

"I have some news of my own. The plot gets thicker. I think Wriedt's grandparents were Helen Van Dale and Tom Cox."

"The madam and the police chief?"

"Exactly. I hit a dead end with one thing, though. The Starck patriarch, Jerry, was also forced to resign, in 1959. From what I read, a few men died while they were in his custody, but the paper didn't give any names. Can you find that out?"

"Should be able to. Let me get going on that right away." I felt like we might finally be closing in on some answers.

34

For all John Looney did to consolidate his power, for all the fear he incited and the friends he paid for, his fall was surprisingly fast. I covered the collapse of Looney's empire in the last chapter of *Too Looney for the Law*.

> Law enforcement finally dropped the hammer on the entirety of the Looney enterprises after the Market Square gunfight in 1922. Within three weeks all of Looney's bars and brothels were closed, his home raided, guns confiscated, and six productive stills were shut down. Later in October, Looney was indicted on federal charges of auto theft and, a couple of months after that, he was also indicted for the murder of Bill Gabel. He had lost most of his property and fortune, his businesses were shut down, and his freedom was the next target. Looney would face a total of ten indictments by the time prosecutors finished filing charges. He fled, hiding in plain sight in his home town of Ottawa, Illinois for several months, but the authorities eventually caught up with him in New Mexico near the end of 1924, more than two years after his son, Connor, was killed at Market Square.
>
> When Looney was brought back to Illinois to

face the charges, the attorney general claimed, incredulously, that the state didn't have the money to take the case to trial. Rock Islanders were not about to lose this battle with Looney, so they organized a campaign that successfully raised the $75,000 needed to prosecute his case. Their cause got a boost from philanthropist and temperance devotee John Hauberg who made a substantial donation; Hauberg had served with the National Guard during the 1912 riot that Looney caused.

The jury was selected from a pool that consisted mostly of people who had contributed to the $75,000 trial fund, a fact that presiding judge Nels Larson apparently wasn't worried might compromise the panel's objectivity. Over the course of five weeks, many of Looney's former associates turned against him and testified about the crime network, detailing how payments were made and how profits were shared.

One of those witnesses was Helen Van Dale, the madam who reigned over the prostitution empire. When asked at the trial why she was testifying, she replied: "After he blackmailed and bled so many people, I think he should have a little justice handed him. If I told all I know about him, I could hang him."

Van Dale didn't say enough to hang Looney, but it didn't matter. On the morning of July 31 the jury returned guilty verdicts for conspiracy to protect gambling, prostitution, and illicit liquor trafficking. Looney barely reacted to the verdict;

he expected it. The jury settled on a sentence of 1-5 years in the state penitentiary, and the judge tacked on another 60 days for contempt of court because Looney carried a gun into the courtroom and called Assistant Attorney General Charles Hadley a liar. Later that day, the *Argus* reprinted an editorial from three years earlier that ended: "With his son gone, Looney is deserted save by those underworld thugs he is paying to shield him in his roost under the hill. He is friendless, as he deserves to be."

Just a few months later, Looney was in court again, this time for the murder of Bill Gabel. The trial was moved to Galesburg at Looney's request; he knew he didn't stand a chance of acquittal from a jury made up of fellow Rock Islanders. Jury selection began on November 23 and dragged on for a week because so many jurors were disqualified. Looney's main defense was that he wasn't even in Rock Island on the night of the murder. The prosecution, led by Senator James Barbour, built a case around circumstantial evidence and the testimony of former associates who had been granted immunity. Barbour's closing argument lasted 7½ hours; Looney's defense team made no closing argument at all.

The jury struggled to reach a verdict—they voted six times before finally reaching unanimity. On the morning of December 23, they announced their decision: guilty, with a recommendation to punish Looney with 14 years in the state penitentiary. The Argus rejoiced at the verdict, proclaiming: "Now we know who killed Bill Gabel...The conviction of John P. Looney is the best Christmas present that justice could have presented to Rock Island and its neighboring cities."

All things considered (like his years of extortion and murder), Looney got off easy. Sure, he lost a son, but he ended up serving less than nine years in prison for all his misdeeds. He was sent to Joliet's Statesville Prison, which was only a year old when he began his sentence on January 9, 1926 as prisoner number 344, one of three thousand inmates at a prison secured by 225 guards. At Statesville he spent much of the time in the hospital with lung problems that wouldn't go away (what would much later be diagnosed as a rare fungal infection). When he wasn't ill, he tended the prison's chickens and gave legal advice to other inmates, even as his own appeals failed one after another. His health declining, although not terminally ill, he was granted an early release in 1934.

On April 7, he walked out of prison, broken and broke. His daughter, Ursula, met him at the prison gate and helped him into the back seat of the car, which she had stuffed with pillows and blankets to make the long ride to Texas easier for him. Only two reporters bothered to show up—in nine years Looney's story had gone from page 1 news to one paragraph in a hack's *Remember When?* column. The reporters tried to get a couple of quotes from Looney or Ursula, but they declined, rushed to the car, and left Illinois, never to return. Looney may have gone away but his legacy would live on.

229

Jefferson only needed a couple of hours to find out the names of the suspects who died while in Jerry Stark's custody: Michael Richards, Ben Ortell, Stephan Ginnane, and Scott Walker. All four, it turned out, were sons of men who were implicated in the murder of Bill Gabel: Joe "The Gadget" Richards, Louis Ortell, Butch Ginnane, and Leonard "Fat" Walker.

"Geez, Brian. I don't mean to denigrate your chosen profession, but those names are right from the Looney era. Did anyone at the time, like another cop maybe, think there might be something fishy going on?"

"Maybe they did, and they just looked the other way, you know, like, maybe they thought those guys got what they had coming to them."

"Maybe; or maybe they were just covering up for another cop until it became too much to hide."

Jerry Starck and his son, Leo, were two generations of vigilante cops. Was it possible that Agent William Starck was the third? Did the Starck family pass along the zeal for retribution like other families hand down grandma's steamer trunk? Even if he didn't kill Miguel, writing about his family history was going to be a lot of fun.

I had spent the whole day at the archives staring at microfilm readers and needed to rest my eyes, so I drove back to the motel and dropped my notes on the dresser. As I moved toward the bed to lie down for a quick nap, I caught a shadow out of the corner of my eye, just a second before I felt something hit the side of my head, knocking me out cold.

35

I don't know how long I was out, but when I woke, it was dark and I couldn't see anything clearly. I could make out some trees and thought I heard water splashing against something. A light breeze blew across my face and my ass was cold and wet. I was pretty sure I wasn't in my motel room; there was never a breeze in that room. I tried to stand up, but got nowhere. I figured out I was sitting on the ground, bound to a tree with ropes around my shoulders, hands tied together in front of me.

The last thing I remembered was that I was about to lie down for a nap. Someone hit me, someone who had been to have been waiting for me in the motel room. Who? I felt my heart pounding faster and faster. After everything I'd been through, all the crazy risks I'd taken in countries around the world, was I going to die in the Quad Cities somewhere in the goddamn woods tied to a tree?

"So you're awake finally." I looked to my right and saw Agent William Starck. "About time you woke up. I didn't hit you that hard." Starck was dressed down, wearing jeans, an Augustana College sweatshirt, and Chicago Cubs baseball cap instead of the polo shirt and slacks I had seen him wearing before.

"What's going on? Where am I?"

"I thought you might recognize this place, but maybe

you didn't have time to take in the sights last time you were here. Over there," he said, pointing to the right, "is where you saw Ramirez floating in the water. I'm still puzzled about what you did that night, Dodge, or what you didn't do. Why did you run off when you saw his body floating in the water? Why didn't you jump in and pull him out? I thought you were a good guy, the hero type, but you're really nothing like that, are you?"

Still trying to figure out what was going on, and still groggy, I couldn't think of anything to say except the truth. "I panicked. He looked dead, and I didn't want to stick around and end up being the next victim."

"So you saved yourself, leaving him to die while you got away."

"He was already dead. There was nothing I could have done."

Starck paused, took off the cap, and ran his fingers through his hair, or what was left of it. He turned to look at the water. "You're probably right, at least about him being dead. I suppose he had been in the water long enough at that point to drown." He put the cap back on and looked down at me. "And I was still here, watching you. Standing over there, in fact," he said, pointing to a large oak tree. "If you'd gone in the water to pull him out, would I have killed you, too? Hard to say. It would have required a change in plans. I suppose I could have turned it into a murder-suicide, but that would have been risky."

I slowly wiggled my shoulders, hoping to find some slack to work with but not getting anywhere. He knew how to tie a rope, I had to give him that. "Why'd you kill

Miguel? What did he ever do to you? Why would you want him dead?"

"It was nothing personal, Dodge. I didn't hate the guy. But he wasn't all you thought he was. He lived his life on the wrong side of the law, on the wrong side of morality, and always would. He came from a rotten seed, and he made a lot of bad choices on top of that. He was just one more crook in a line of crooks. If I didn't stop him now, he would have done something worse later and someone would suffer because of it. He couldn't help it. It's in his blood, so he had to go." A gust of wind blew across the island; Starck grabbed the top of his head to keep his cap from blowing off.

"Miguel got caught bringing pot into the country. That's all. How does that make him a lifelong crook?"

"You think this is just about pot? You really don't know Miguel at all do you? He didn't just run drugs a couple of times. He was part of a network that distributed just about any kind of drug you can imagine."

I assumed that Miguel had only transported marijuana. I felt confused, not sure if it should matter what drugs he transported or what that might say about him. Had he lied to me? Maybe I just didn't ask the right questions. I had a good feeling about Miguel, about the kind of person he was—honorable, smart, remorseful—and I didn't think I was wrong. "Does it really matter, Starck, if Miguel transported other drugs, too?" I stammered. "He was just a driver and not a willing one at that."

"Oh, I see," Starck said, looking just a little too happy. "He didn't tell you the whole story, did he? I'm not surprised. He didn't excel at accepting responsibility. Let me fill in the details that Ramirez left out. The FBI had been watching him for a few months. We had a tip that he was repaying a debt by driving trucks across the border from Mexico, bringing drugs into the US. He'd gotten in trouble in McAllen when he borrowed too much money from folks who don't usually think of themselves as bankers. Ramirez was a terrible gambler, as you saw firsthand. They could have just killed him, but they figured they could use him to get some of that money back. He was a college kid with no record, US-born, clean cut, spoke English and Spanish well. They put him to work as a driver to move product across the border."

"I know about that, more or less. He told me. Cody was blackmailing him to keep his mouth shut. You're just making my point for me: he wasn't a crook at heart."

"To pay off his debt, he agreed to drive a truck across the border twice a week, semis usually, loaded with TVs or car parts or something like that, with packages of marijuana, coke, heroin, meth, whatever, hidden in strategic places; like I said, pretty much any drug you can imagine. He'd been doing it for at least six months before we were tipped off. He was good at it, even helped plan the routes and figured out new ways to hide the drugs he carried. We watched for a while, trying to figure out how connected he really was. The day we finally moved on him, he was driving a semi with a trailer fully loaded with shoes and shirts and a false wall. The compartment hid a stash of drugs, a hundred kilos of pot on that trip."

"Again, I know this story."

"You just don't get it, Dodge. He brought drugs into this country, a lot of drugs, and not just a little pot so college kids and old hippies could get high, but drugs like meth and heroin that ruined communities; drugs that could, and probably did, kill people." Another gust of wind blew suddenly, grabbing the Cubs hat off Starck's head and dropping it into the slough. He looked like he was about to jump in the water to save the hat, but he stayed put. "Damn. I loved that hat," he said as he watched it float away.

Turning back to me, he continued, "Did Ramirez mention that he also transported guns? Those same trucks were sometimes loaded with handguns and automatic rifles. But this wasn't just about drugs or guns; it was about the bigger picture. Ramirez was part of a cartel that destroyed lives, hundreds, if not thousands, of lives. And he chose to be a part of it. Sure, he backed into it by piling up gambling debt, but how do you think that happened? He wasn't throwing away change on the slots in a Vegas-type casino. He was playing poker in an underground, and illegal, network, betting against drug dealers, thieves, and other low-lifes. He sought them out, knew who he was playing against, and, once he was forced to work for them, he embraced it, he fucking embraced working with them," he nearly screamed, "because he wanted to be a gangster like his father and grandfather." Starck took a couple of steps back. "But he got in over his head. When we busted him, he dropped his loyalties quicker than, well, quicker than he emptied your bank account at the casino. He was more worried about his own ass—like you—and begged us to go easy, to make a deal."

"Even after he had been busted and after he moved

up here to Davenport, he couldn't keep himself out of trouble. He stole drugs from that roommate of his, Cody, then turned around and sold them so he could have some spare cash. Sometimes he even sold to Cody's own customers. He even had the nerve to double the price when supplies ran short in the region for a while. That bartender you met had to pay Ramirez twice the price he normally got from Hahn, for pot that Ramirez stole from Hahn. He was no angel, Dodge, and, in the end, he did what any good crook does—he scrambled to cover his own ass at the expense of everyone else. Again, like you."

I felt let down by Miguel after hearing Starck. I couldn't help it. It was easier to think of him as a victim or a pawn than someone who was in the thicket by choice. "You could be right, Starck, about Miguel." I could barely speak. "Maybe he wanted to be a crook, at least in the beginning. Maybe he heard stories about his family's crimes and it sounded romantic to him. He was a kid, probably didn't have any idea what he was really getting himself into, what it could cost him. Hell, even when I met him, he was still trying to figure out who he was. But even if you're right, he deserved better than what you gave him. He felt remorse about what he did. I'm sure of it. He knew he wasn't cut out for the gangster life and was turning things around. So why kill him? And why now? Is this some kind of twisted family tradition that you swore to carry on?"

"I heard you've been poking around my family's business."

"Speaking of crooks and cowards…" I mumbled.

Starck took a step in my direction, right fist clenched,

but stopped himself. "You're a fool, Dodge. You can't understand what my family has been through. We were the victims. Bill Gabel was executed by Looney's gang because he tried to turn Looney in; Gabel was killed for doing the right thing. We honor his sacrifice by aspiring to live our lives with the same dignity and moral clarity that he lived his."

"You have a gift for rewriting history, Starck. Bill Gabel was killed because he was greedy. He was just trying to make more money for himself and less for Looney, a simple business calculation by a man trying to out-crook the master crook, Looney. Gabel gave up on being a cop so he could get rich, but he had to make a deal with the devil to make it happen. So he made the deal. And when he wasn't happy with the terms anymore, he turned into a rat and gave evidence to the feds, hoping they could void the contract. When Gabel went after the devil, the devil had to foreclose on his soul; he had no other choice. Gabel was no more a victim than John Looney. He was just another crook."

I guess that was too much for Starck. He came at me quickly and hit me with the butt of his pistol—enough with the head already!—knocking everything hazy for a few minutes. When everything around me stopped spinning, I saw Starck standing a few feet in front of me, staring down. Raising his right arm, moonlight flashed across the gun barrel as he wiped his brow with a shirtsleeve.

I've never been good at keeping my mouth shut, and I wasn't about to stop just because I was tied to a tree. "I still don't understand how any of this justifies killing

Miguel. Or why it's OK for your grandfather to kill four men. Or why your father can get away with killing a man in cold blood. And all of the Starck family victims are connected to Gabel's killers. It looks like your family was on a mission to wipe out everyone who had a connection to the men who killed Gabel, a lust for vengeance that was passed from father to son to grandson. That's what you call moral clarity?"

"You don't get it at all, Dodge. We didn't kill just anyone from those families; we were just pruning the bad wood, getting rid of the troublemakers. You can look it up; well, actually, you won't be able to, because I'm going to kill you, so you'll have to take my word for it. All those men had records. My grandfather wasn't very patient. After all, he was very close to it all, seeing as he was Bill Gabel's son. He killed anyone from those families who was accused of a crime; he didn't wait for a court to decide if they were guilty. My father and me, we've been more careful. Dad wasn't going to kill Wriedt; he had been watching him for a long time and warning him to clean up his act. Dad gave him a beating a few times after the petty robberies and drunken bar fights that Wriedt just couldn't stay away from. But when Wriedt fondled a little girl, that was too much. My dad had to act. Just like I had to act with Ramirez. Honestly, I didn't know I was going to kill him until he started selling—and stealing—drugs after moving to Davenport. At that point, I knew that Ramirez had to go."

"People like Ramirez don't change, Dodge. They may sometimes act like they feel guilty, and maybe they really do, for a little while, but it doesn't last and it's never enough to get them to change who they are or what they do. They never change, Dodge. Never. Ramirez's actions killed people, maybe not directly, but just as certainly. I know it. If I didn't act, more people would have died because of him. But I had to wait for the right chance. I'm not going to lose my job like my dad and granddad did."

The picture was coming into focus now. "So you decided to frame me for his murder."

"Yes. You were a gift, a sign from God even. I'd been trying to figure out a way to get rid of Ramirez, but I hadn't landed on the right idea, yet. Then I met your friend, the homicide cop, at a conference. After my talk, he asked me a bunch of questions about the history of organized crime, especially Looney. He really wanted to know if Looney had any living relatives, and mentioned how he and his writer friend wondered if any of John Looney's descendants had gotten involved in organized crime, too."

"After he left, I realized that I had an opportunity. I saw him later that evening in the lobby, so I tipped him off about Ramirez. The FBI was about done with Ramirez by then. He'd given us names and wore a wire for a couple of deals. We got most of the key players in the Texas gang he was working for, and we got all the information we were going to get on his contacts in Mexico. I told him to move away from Texas, to start over, and suggested he come here, that I had some contacts who could help him out. I really just wanted to keep him in my sights, so I could move when I was ready."

"So you planned the whole thing with me and Miguel?"

"Yes and no. I made up most of it along the way. It helped that you friended Ramirez on Facebook. I'd been watching his profile for a while, monitoring his friends and what he was doing. Then you showed up, rather, Steve Smith showed up, but it wasn't hard to figure out that Smith was a front for you. And that opened a door for me."

"I told Ramirez that I needed him to do one more act of penance for the FBI, that a guy was coming to the Quad Cities who we thought was going to try to move a lot of product, that he would say he was a writer, and that we had a tip that he was going to use the Crooked Spine as a base. Then I sent him a picture of you, from your real Facebook profile."

"Clever. And here I thought it was a coincidence when he sat down next to me."

"I don't believe in coincidence; I believe in control. I kept in contact with Ramirez through the night, sending him text messages to make sure he stayed with you. When you went to the casino, I knew I was going to get a chance to make something happen. So I told Ramirez to go join you, to borrow money from you and to encourage you to make bigger and bigger bets. I knew he was a lousy gambler and you'd probably go broke. Then I gave him the drug deal cover story to get you both to Suiter Park."

"I underestimated you, Starck. You did all that on the fly? So what's your cover story going to be for killing me?"

"That's easy. Suicide. Given your history, you're not exactly a stable guy. And the police just put you in jail for a night on suspicion of murder. You were depressed and alone, no real connections to anyone, so you caved to the pressure and decided to do yourself in at the spot where you killed Ramirez. You have a flair for the dramatic, I think."

I didn't doubt him when he said he was going to kill me. I needed to keep him talking, do some fishing and stall for a while until I could come up with a way out, an escape plan. "Doesn't killing me break your family code, or whatever the fuck vigilantes call it? I don't have any family ties to Bill Gabel's murder. I'm not even from here. Killing me doesn't make you a hero on a noble quest, it makes you a common criminal."

"I don't see it that way, Dodge. Sometimes sacrifices have to be made for the greater good. I need to be able to continue my work, my family's work, to do my part to prevent these crooks from hurting more people, but I won't be able to do that if the cops figure out that I killed Ramirez. So for me to carry on, you have to go, too. It's pretty simple, really. Your death will ensure the safety of many others. You should feel good about that."

"You can rationalize it any way you want, but you're just out to save your own ass, like you accused Miguel and me of doing. There's nothing noble about that."

"If I don't survive, neither does the mission. Now, enough talking. I still have a lot of work to do, and I don't have all night. Open wide."

I squirmed frantically, trying to loosen the ropes but they just wouldn't budge. As Starck moved toward me and pointed the gun, I closed my eyes and thought about Miguel, Anna Hanks, Joe Malone, my sister, my parents, and all the other friends and family who died before me. I wondered what I would be feeling if I believed in an afterlife, at least until my thoughts were interrupted by the pop of a gun firing and a warm, wet splatter across my face.

36

"Frank. Frank. You OK?" I heard a familiar voice. Maybe there is an afterlife. Maybe that's where I was. "Frank—talk to me." The voice sounded like it was right next to me. I felt someone loosening the ropes around my shoulders. I blinked a couple of times, opening my eyes slowly and looking around. Jefferson was kneeling next to me, and Starck was on the ground in front of me, blood oozing out of his head.

"Frank. Talk to me." Jefferson's hands were trembling and his breathing was fast and shallow.

"What happened?" I stammered. "I thought karma had finally caught up with me."

"I've got your back, remember?" He worked the rest of the ropes free. "Are you OK? I thought I was gonna lose you, brother."

"My head hurts like hell and my ass is cold, but I'm alive. Thanks to you," I said, closing my eyes and rubbing my forehead. "How did you find me?"

"A little luck and a lot of good police work," Jefferson said.

"When you didn't answer my calls earlier this evening, I wasn't too concerned, not at first. I know you can get lost in your work. You always get back to me, though; always. After spending most of my day combing through files and talking to people who knew the Starcks, I still hadn't heard from you. I got worried. So I went back to the motel around ten and saw that your car was still there. I pounded on your door and you didn't answer, so I got the manager to open the door and let me in. I didn't like what I saw: your laptop on the floor, car keys on the dresser, and pieces of rope on the floor. I was really bothered by the pieces of rope. I knew you were in trouble, that someone had probably knocked you out and taken you away, and I was pretty sure it was Starck. I didn't have much time to find you, so I took a chance that he had taken you back to Suiter Park. It was a guess, but I figured he wanted to set you up as the one who killed Ramirez, and I hoped that his plans involved going back to where Ramirez died."

"A lucky guess? That's all that was between me and death?"

"Good police work and a good guess," he emphasized. "We found Noah in the early evening. He'd been camping on an island in the Mississippi, fishing and getting high; didn't even know that Cody had been arrested. Once he got to talking, we were pretty sure that he and Cody hadn't killed Ramirez, so that's when I was convinced it had to be Starck."

"How'd you find me here, in this spot?"

"It wasn't easy. It was dark, and, like you said, there are a lot of trails on this island. It was spooky, man. I'd rather search for someone in an abandoned building than here in these woods. Something's just wrong about this place. Anyway, I remembered the direction you said you walked, the night Ramirez was killed, and went the same way, to the left after crossing the bridge. I had my gun out and ready, prepared to shoot any fucking thing that got in my way, but trying hard not to be too jumpy; I didn't want to be shooting at shadows or tree trunks. The wind was picking up, so that wasn't so easy."

"As I got close to the water's edge, I thought I heard voices, faint ones, but I was pretty sure they were voices. So I slowed down, hiding behind tree trunks for cover. Something began to take shape just ahead of me, someone standing a few feet away with his back to me. He was looking down, talking to someone that I couldn't see. As I crept closer, the guy looked around, turning his head to the left and the right; that's when I realized it was Agent Starck. By then I was close enough to make out the voices, so I knew he was talking to you, but I still couldn't see where you were. Then I saw Starck's gun and where he was pointing it, and I figured you had to be on the other end, on the ground, probably tied up. I knew what I had to do. I steadied myself, took aim, and as he was lifting his gun toward you, I fired."

"You just shot him? You didn't think about trying to take him alive?" I asked.

"No. Not for a second. Not for one second. Hey, I better call Martens and get some help out here."

After he hung up, Jefferson turned back to me. I was still reeling from everything. He pulled out his handkerchief and started to wipe the blood off my face.

"For some reason I'm having a flashback to how we met," I said, in between swipes.

"You were getting your ass kicked by four other kids."

"Just another day at school for me. But that day, something different happened, someone jumped in to help me."

"It was my first day at that school."

"Yeah. It was your first day, and you were just about the only black kid in the whole school, and what do you do to make an impression? You get in the middle of some bullies picking on a nerd and rescue the nerd."

"I have a thing about looking out for the little guys. What can I say?"

"You did it well. You gave all four of them something to remember, like bruises and black eyes."

"And I got a quick vacation, too. The principal wasn't as thrilled as you were, so she gave me a few days off at home to think about what I'd done and whether I was a good fit for that school. And when I came back, you had copies of your class notes ready for me and spent a few hours after school helping me catch up."

"I was no fool," I said. "I may be now, but I wasn't then. No one else looked out for me at that school; I was going to make sure I kept you in my corner. I'd say it worked. I don't think I can ever pay you back for what you've done, Brian, especially for tonight."

"Ah, shut the fuck up. You've helped me a lot, too, I just don't go on about it like you do. You know I wouldn't be here today if you hadn't stuck with me, too. Pushed me to get through classes when I was bored; kept me from getting too discouraged while I courted my future wife. You can travel all you want, but you'll always be a big part of my life. I wasn't about to let some fucked up FBI fool end that."

"So we're still going to be talking after this?"

"Of course! Why wouldn't we?"

"I don't know. I guess I thought I'd gone too far this

time, that you had had enough of trying to rescue me."

"Hell, no. I won't lie; you did go too far this time, and you came damn close to an ugly end. But I wouldn't give up on you. What would I do if I didn't have someone who actually needed my help? I've got a wife who wants to leave me and two teenage daughters, Frank. The wife doesn't need me for anything anymore and my girls, all they want from me is a car to drive and some cash to spend. But you, you're in trouble all the time, real trouble; you actually need my help. And this was a helluva lot of fun," Jefferson laughed, then caught himself. "Don't get me wrong; I know how close we were to having this all end very badly...but goddamn it was fun."

By the time the EMTs, beat cops, detectives, special agents, and reporters showed up, Jefferson had cleaned off most of the blood from my face and was helping me stand up. We told them, the law enforcement folks, anyway, why an FBI agent was lying on the ground with a sizeable hole in his head.

Jefferson's decision to shoot first and explain later wasn't universally well-received. He had to defend his action to a few detectives, talk down some pissed off FBI agents, and avoid the press. In the end, no one had the will, or any evidence of wrong-doing, to charge him with anything.

It helped that there was little doubt that Agent Starck killed Miguel. The Moline police discovered that Starck rented an efficiency apartment in downtown Rock Island. When they searched it, they found a set of elaborate family trees going back to the 1920s, charts for John Looney, Louis Ortell, Leonard Walker, Charles Gin-

247

nane, Joe Richards, and Tom Cox, all of the men who were implicated in the murder of Bill Gabel. Each chart showed marriages, children, and grandchildren. Next to each name, Starck had scribbled notes: deceased, clean, or rotten. Every name that had been marked "rotten" had a red "X" through it: victims I expected to find like Michael Richards, Ben Ortell, Stephan Ginnane, Scott Walker, and Miguel, but also a couple of surprises: Ted Ortell and Chuck Richards, men who had died in the past five years and whose deaths had been ruled suicides. The page that began with John Looney had boxes printed for each of his children. From one side, a new box had been written in by hand for Lupina Ramirez, showing her with a son, Juan Ramirez, and another box for her grandson, Miguel Ramirez, marked with a red "X" through it.

Agent Starck had kept Miguel's backpack, which he had stuffed into a closet. Inside the backpack, police found Miguel's phone, a few chiropractic textbooks, Doyle Brunson's Super System: A Course in Power Poker, a couple of pictures of his mother, and a copy of *Too Looney for the Law* still wrapped securely in plastic.

I called Ruby to let her know that everything was OK, but I left out a few details, like the kidnapping and a gun in my face, although she'd probably read about t of that in the paper later. I'd tell her more of the the next time I saw her.

37

John Looney lived in the headlines, but his death went almost unnoticed. Just eight years after leaving prison, John Looney died in southern Texas, killed by a lung infection and a touch of senility. Some might say he'd been suffering from both for most of his life. On the death certificate, Looney's occupation was listed as "retired rancher", which I guess is what passes for a gangster in Texas. Looney was buried in Rose Lawn Cemetery in McAllen, Texas, 1,500 miles from where he grew up and the streets he once ruled. In spite of the chronic lung infection, the frail body, the multiple beatings, and the multiple assassination attempts, he lived 75 years. Miguel's life complemented Looney's: born in Texas and buried in Rock Island, Miguel, a tough young man, lived a robust but short life, while Looney's was painfully long.

The coroner determined that Miguel had drowned, that the blow to the head had knocked him out but wasn't fatal. He was still alive when his body was dumped in the water. Could I have saved him that night if I'd pulled his body from the water? Maybe; maybe not. Starck's fingerprints were all over Miguel's phone. Jefferson and I believe that Starck actually sent the last text to me, not Miguel, which would mean Miguel was certainly dead when I saw his body floating in the slough. But, I'll never really know. I suppose it doesn't matter. Starck made it clear that he was hiding in the woods that night. If I had fished out Miguel's body and tried to revive him, Starck would have made sure we were both dead.

By the time Miguel Ramirez was buried on Thursday morning at Chippiannock Cemetery, a strong north wind had blown away the early spring warmth. I suppose Chippiannock was an appropriate resting place for Miguel. Looney's wife and son are buried in the adjacent Calvary Cemetery, although no one is certain just where. They didn't get grand send-offs or marble headstones; in fact, they didn't get markers at all. Some speculate that Looney himself was buried next door in Calvary Cemetery, too, rather than in Texas. No one will be visiting his grave, anyway, because his plot doesn't have a marker, either.

For Miguel, though, it will be different: anyone who passes by will know that a Miguel Ramirez lived a life that ended too soon: born 1988, died 2012. He will have a dignified granite marker carved with his full name.

As his casket was lowered into the vault, I pulled my coat tighter and said a quiet goodbye. Afterwards, my plans to make a quick escape were frustrated when an elderly man wearing a black suit approached me.

"Are you Frank Dodge, the writer?"

"That's me," I mumbled.

"I'm Juan Ramirez." He reached out to shake my hand. "Miguel was my son. I was told that you were the last person to see him alive, that you were his friend."

"I'm so sorry for what happened to him. If only I'd known his life was in danger, maybe I could have done something to stop it. He was a good kid."

"Yes. He was a good kid, most of the time. He deserved better than he got. I know he deserved a better father."

"I don't think that's true at all. He loved and admired you. He just wished you could have spent more time together."

"That's kind of you to say. The thing is, I always had a troubled relationship with the truth, but it was Miguel who paid the price for it. His death is my fault," he said, looking toward the open grave.

"I don't follow."

"From the time I was little, I remember my mom telling stories about John Looney and his family, and all the trouble he created, stories she picked up by working for his family for so long. It was easy to believe that Looney was my dad, and I understood why someone like him wouldn't want to admit it. It just made me want to be like him even more, to prove I was his kin."

"I'm not sure Looney really cared about what other people thought, but the rest of the family probably did," I said.

Juan looked down and nodded. "When I was in high school, John Looney was dead a long time by then, I asked my mom about their relationship. How she met him, did they think about getting married, that kind of thing. She just stared at me and screamed 'What are you talking about? Relationship? What relationship? I was his housekeeper.'

"'But you were his lover, too, right? He was my father, so you must have thought about getting married at some point,' I asked her."

"'What are you talking about Juanito? I never told you that. Mr. Looney gave me a job, not a baby. He was not your father, hijo. Your father was a ranch hand who worked for Mr. Looney for the summer. When I was pregnant with you, he told me he already had a wife and family back in Arizona and didn't need another one. Then he left us. I was so hurt, and naïve. When you were born, I refused to put his name on your birth certificate. I didn't want to give that man any chance of coming back and doing any more harm.'"

"I'm confused," I interrupted. "Are you saying that John Looney wasn't your father at all? That Miguel wasn't John Looney's grandson?" I asked, feeling more than a little irritated.

"Yeah," Juan replied, keeping his gaze fixed on the ground.

"So why did you tell Miguel that he was?"

"I thought it would impress him, to know the kind of tough people that he came from, that his papa couldn't be such a loser if his father was a famous gangster. I didn't mean anything bad by it. I would have told him the truth some day, but I kept putting it off because it seemed real important to him to believe it." Juan finally looked back up at me. "I let him down most of his life. I was afraid that if he knew the truth, that we weren't related to John Looney, it would be the last time he'd take disappointment from me."

"I don't know what to tell you, Mr. Ramirez. I'm sorry. Just sorry." I turned to look at him, but I couldn't take looking in his eyes, all the regret and shame on the verge of exploding; I quickly looked away. I reached in my

252

pocket and pulled out Miguel's silver necklace. I turned
it over a couple of times in my hand, then gave it to Mr.
Ramirez. "I think Miguel would want you to have this."
I shook his hand, patted him on the shoulder, and walked
away.

After the burial, the college hosted a memorial service
for Miguel, which drew a bigger crowd than I expected.
A lot of students from Dickey turned out to say good-bye
to one of their own and to play a role in a tragedy. The
rest of the day was slow, not enough work to keep me
busy. With all that idle time, I thought a lot about Miguel,
surprised at the depth of my grief, as if I had lost a good
friend, someone that I had known all my life. I had to
remind myself that I only knew him for that one night.

Epilogue

I got back in St. Louis in time for Anna Hanks' memorial service. Two funerals in two days. I told Jefferson about my conversation with Miguel's father, that Miguel wasn't related to Looney at all. He took it more in stride than I did. He was used to being on the margins of tragedies. It was just part of his job. I was still trying to get used to living in one. "I'm just glad we got your name cleared and got you out of there alive. Maybe now you'll listen to me more often, and you'll be more careful."

Jefferson didn't like to admit it, but he had a lot of dreamer in him.

All things considered, Jefferson and I got out of this mess without much damage. Sure, he and Michelle ended up divorcing, but that seemed inevitable. By the time Jefferson got home, Michelle had moved out. He didn't seem surprised. I helped as I could, but he wasn't looking for much, just someone to carry a few boxes so he could set up his new place more quickly. He seemed resigned to the end of the marriage and put his energy into figuring out how he was going to see his girls every day. That part ended up being simple. Michelle got a place nearby, so it was easy for the girls to go back and forth.

He lost points at work for killing an FBI agent, an act that is generally frowned upon even when justified, especially if you work in law enforcement. Jefferson will survive, though. He'll probably make sergeant soon in spite of it.

Cody Hahn is sitting in jail, not for blackmailing Miguel, the extent of which turned out to be nothing more than making Miguel buy his drinks and pay his rent, but for federal charges of drug trafficking. If he'd stuck to selling in Iowa alone, he probably would have gotten a few months in the Scott County jail and a long probation. But he didn't. He sold in both Iowa and Illinois, and he was a jerk, so the Moline cops turned him over to the FBI, token compensation for losing one of their own. Cody will be locked up for a few years now. Noah pled guilty to a misdemeanor drug charge, and lost his job at the Crooked Spine. He left town to look for a bartending job upriver, somewhere in Wisconsin, I heard.

As for me, my head still hurts but it will heal. I ended up with a very different story than I went in search of. John Looney had blurred the lines between good and evil, turning good men bad with the promise of easy money and power: mayors, police, lawyers, and regular folks took the bait and mixed their fortunes intimately with those of ruthless killers and shameless opportunists. The Quad Cities, but Rock Island especially, became defined by the lawlessness and immorality and few were untouched by it.

The Starck family was touched more than most. They took a lesson from Looney and adopted his tactics of intimidation and violence; they just thought they were using it for a more noble purpose: to rid the world of criminals who had the DNA of Bill Gabel's killers in their blood. But Agent Starck killed an innocent man.

Sure, Miguel Ramirez made some bad decisions, but crime wasn't going to be his life. And he wasn't even part of the Looney legacy, at least not directly.

That's what I ended up writing, a story about family legacies and how the hunger for vengeance can be passed down a family tree. It's a good story, one of my best, I think. I'm still trying to find someone to publish it. On the other hand, my piece called "A Brewpub for Every Palate" ran last week in the *St. Louis Post-Dispatch*.

Dean Klinkenberg, the Mississippi Valley Traveler, explores the back roads and backwaters of the Mississippi River Valley, a place with an abundance of stories to tell, big characters, epic struggles, do-gooders and evil-doers. Some of those stories are in the Frank Dodge mystery series; others you'll find in the Mississippi Valley Traveler guidebooks. He lives in St. Louis with his husband, John, and a parrot, Ra. *Rock Island Lines* is his first novel.

www.MississippiValleyTraveler.com
@MissValleyTrav